BEFORE THEY REMEMBER

RAYNA ARORA

notionpress.com

INDIA • SINGAPORE • MALAYSIA

ISBN 979-8-89026-487-9

Contents

Part 1
The Past

Chapter 1	The Town of Abilo	7
Chapter 2	Aunt Brie's Tale	13
Chapter 3	The Lake's Light	20
Chapter 4	Betty Harbour the Fugitive	26
Chapter 5	Playback on Kipsy City	31
Chapter 6	The Tunnel of Memories	38
Chapter 7	Golden Gateway to Another Mystery	46
Chapter 8	The Rotating Liah	53
Chapter 9	Patrick's Pool Party	59
Chapter 10	In Sickness and in Feigned Love	69
Chapter 11	Asylum Therapy	77
Chapter 12	Back at Brie's	85
Chapter 13	The Fear of Remembering	89

Part 2
The Present

Chapter 14	Salt Lake	101
Chapter 15	Explosions	109
Chapter 16	The Game	118
Chapter 17	Snakes & Ladders	126
Chapter 18	The Real Snakes & The Real Ladders	136
Chapter 19	The Winning Indifferent	146
Chapter 20	Aftermath	153
Chapter 21	Hopeless Light	164
Chapter 22	Levian or Grayson	173
Chapter 23	Larson's Stables & Farm	179
Chapter 24	The Cycle	184
Chapter 25	A Moment of Calm	191
Chapter 26	Water Portals	198
Chapter 27	Goodbye Esme	207

Part 3
The Future

Chapter 28	The Levian Chapter	215

Part 1

The Past

CHAPTER 1

The Town of Abilo

A town with few people filled with provincial beliefs, stiff imagination, and mechanical ways of a construct is the land of my bloom. When I was born, my mother who was raised by witches decided to bless her baby with powers of aquatic freedom and magic or as the towns folk would say, a mermaid. She wanted me to know that I was always loved and christened me Esmerliah, a name that was perceived as the esteemed mermaid. I always loved hearing this little fable because after my mother died when I was only a mere toddler, I was orphaned with no evidence of my past in the town of Abilo but the stories were convivial, especially the way my aunt would tell them.

Why am I writing this? Well, actually it's just a memory I want to store for myself later in case I ever get into another accident or have my memory completely wiped as in my experience it's hard for the people around you to deal with you when you remember nothing from your past. My mind is so fogged up even now that every day I breathe, I have to constantly refresh my memory so I remember my life in the randomized scraps of events I can recall, how I felt in every moment however is an entirely different ball game so bear with me as I indulge you with my past, my present and possibly my hopes for the future so I can remind myself of the feelings I had unless of course, I can get someone to write me a biography then my future is left to them. It sounds like a beautiful pick-up line, if I were ever to fall in love with someone, he would continue writing about my future which would be his and his alone… Well back to the story of the first few experiences I have in my distorted life. Back to Abilo!

Yes, the people are good to me here but there is something decidedly amiss about the Abilonians as they are called. Whenever I pass the town's local shop or get ice-cream for myself, the people would give me frightened glares before they scurry off. I have always pondered upon whether they have a distaste for vagrants like me or simply lack the ardent attitude that townsfolk should possess. I was sauntering barefoot in the Abilo park, my lacy feathered dress trailing behind me, its pink and purple ruffles rustling against the swishing sound of the trees against the light breeze that hung on the spring sky. I loved spring, it brought out the fairy tale life in me and I could almost taste the sparkly scent of the lukewarm air as I ran across the park, my red tresses flowing behind me.

"Esme! Come back here you naughty child!", called a huffy voice in the distance and my tranquil dream was broken as I sullenly made my way back to the little cottage that I lived in with my Aunt Brie. "You're half an hour late to tea, where on earth did you go?", she demanded, her hands on her hips. I faked looking as dejected as possible and sheepishly replied, "I'm sorry Aunt Brie, I was in the park". For someone who has never had children of her own, my aunt plays the part of a worried mother rather frequently and the worry lines across her forehead illustrate her obsession with ruining young girls' fun. She scrutinized my rather pretentious demeanour and shook her head violently, eyes bulging. "Esme, please tell me you did not go for a dip into that pool", said she with an unnecessary amount of trepidation. I shook my head truthfully and replied, "Aunty Brie, I'm genuinely sorry for being late but I just got lost in my thoughts today and it was such a deliciously cool day today, I just had to!". Brie must have considered this apology as heartfelt because she said no more and only gave me a disapproving glare as she set the lemon tarts and scones into tiny little plates, pouring my tea for me before she patted her chair down and sank into it.

There was silence for a while as I graciously sipped my tea and ate my tarts in silence. I love tea times because usually my aunt and I would first exchange random poems we came up with and then chat about all the events that happened to us today or the new oddity I had seen in the town from the people who would walk away from me. She was the only person who would interact with me without flinching or looking scared, it was maddening but so relieving at the same time. My eyes flitted back to her face which was turned towards the window away from me. A knife could cut through the silence and still take two slashes. "Are you upset?", I inquired unable to bear the discomfiture any longer. The latter didn't respond. "Did something happen, Brie?", I tried again searchingly, attempting to read her inexpressive face. "Not really darling, drink your tea", she answered. "It's like interrogating a wall", I murmured unsure of what to say as I gobbled down my scones. "The Abilo adoption agency called today", she said at last looking at me, I always loved her piercing blue eyes and the way they twinkled when they faced me. "Why, are you adopting another child?", I joked but she didn't seem so jovial. "They wanted to know about your whereabouts and they decided they want to meet you". I was taken aback by this news, the Abilo adoption agency never called houses or met children unless there was a tragic incident happening. The last time I heard about them was when the cake shop girl Cassy gave birth to her baby and didn't want a child. Cassy was also a rare instance where someone would take to me normally. "Okaaay…", I said flabbergasted. "They're not going to make me leave you, are they?" My Aunt got very emotional just then. "Esme honey, nobody can do that, you are my family and you always will be no matter what", she said firmly and kissed my forehead. "Now run off and play and don't be late to supper".

I smiled and decided to forget about the issue for a little while and slipped into my boots and trotted outside into the dark to go get some ice cream for myself. Subconsciously, I was aware that I wanted to see Cassy and ask her about the agency but I tread lightly and slowly not knowing what to make out of this day. Suddenly, I hear a whinnying noise in the distance on my way to the cake shop and I followed the sound of its voice inquisitively. It sounded like an animal in pain and the clip-clop of hooves made me want to go help it. I adored animals, horses, dogs and birds. whichever animal came by, they were the only friends I could make in this town to who I would tell stories. They were never scared of me.

I followed the noise into a dark alleyway, the protruding sounds of only twigs snapping beneath my boots petrifying me a little. I couldn't hear the horse anymore and I no longer recognized this part of Abilo. "Oh dear, I'm in hot water again if I don't find my way back", I sighed out loud as the noise stopped. "Ooooff!", gushed the sound again and I ran in the direction of it finally reaching at a little clearing where a tiny lake glistened reflecting the moon. A tall, brown horse with the softest brown eyes stood in front of the lake. She was pawing anxiously at the ground with her hooves and seemed to be rearing in pain. "Hello, I'm Esmerliah", I said introducing myself to her before stroking her mane gently. "What's wrong?", I asked her as she pawed the ground again beseechingly. I frowned, her hoof was acting odd and then I noticed a giant splinter stuck on her hoof. "Stand still, I'll get it out", I said soothingly and proceeded to pull the splinter out trying my best to keep her steady. It was a dreadful splinter and took all of my concentration to get it out the relief on her face was rewarding as she nuzzled across my shoulder in thanks before leaving the clearing. I grinned and looked at the lake wistfully.

My aunt never let me swim in it and I really wanted to. All her stories about my name and the water just sounded so very captivating. I looked around cautiously. "One little dip can't hurt anyone", I said to myself convincingly and pulled off my boots dipping my feet into the water. It was the best feeling in the world, the water tickled the soles of my feet making me giggle. I lowered myself into the lake, the cool water pulling me inside like a drug and I floated on my back, laughing as I enjoyed my new centre of gravity. I grabbed handfuls of water in my outstretched arms to splash myself and I could feel a weird sensation as I did so. Every time, I ran my hand through the water, a light beamed out of the pool with the same feeling. “What is that”, I thought, immediately getting distracted by the sounds of deep voices drawing close to the lake. “Oh no, I’m so getting in trouble”, I sighed.

CHAPTER 2

Aunt Brie's Tale

"We found her close to the Abilo tunnel, she was flailing about in a lake close to it", said the sturdy voice of Inspector Kingsley as he roughly pulled my arm forward to show my shameful demeanour to Aunt Brie. I looked behind and glared at the policemen behind him, they bore no malice but just stared unblinkingly at my aunt's cottage door and I stuck my tongue out at them childishly. My luck seemed to despise me and favour trouble because the voices I heard very aggravatingly had to be the Inspector of Abilo and his policemen. I looked at my aunt imploringly, silently begging her for forgiveness but her quivering eye twitch told me otherwise. "Thank you, officer, I'll take care this doesn't happen again", she assured the police officers ushering them out of the cottage before facing me with a look of pure fury although I could see a glint of disappointment too in her eye.

"I didn't mean to Brie", I said hanging my head realising it was a mistake as soon as the words fell out of my lips. "This is where you stop talking!", she said now, her eyes bulging out, wide and menacing. "I gave you one rule Esmerliah, *do not* go out late and *do not* run off in the dark". "Technically, that's two", I corrected her enabling a shriek of rage from my guardian. "What is the matter with you? Do you want to die? You almost left the town, you have no idea what horrors present outside Abilo are, yet you had the imprudence to jump into a lake!", she said brandishing her finger around like a wand which I could tell was hexing me. My aunt was a prepossessing woman with gorgeous red locks of hair and the brightest eyes I had ever seen but right now she resembled the caricature of a devil with a blotchy nose and I could have sworn I saw her horns sticking out at one point.

My head was buzzing now with the constant yelling of my aunt and my tired legs chose that very moment to droop and I fell to my knees. Brie helped me up still looking angry but she stopped yelling although the tight grasp of my arm didn't make it better. "I'm sorry really, but I don't get why you won't let me go into the water if my name is Esmerliah and you telling me all those stories doesn't help me stay away, irony it really is". Brie looked thoughtful for a moment and then said, "I know darling I do, I'm just trying to protect you and you'll have to trust me". This made my blood turn cold and I wrenched myself out of her arms and said, "You can't just not tell me anything about me, I mean what's going on Brie? First, it's the people at Abilo who look at me like I'm a heinous sorcerer, then it's the adoption agency coming who has never actually been seen before and now this! I'm seventeen for heaven's sake, I deserve to know the truth you're hiding from me". I was shivering uncontrollably after my sudden outburst but I couldn't tell whether it was because of swimming in ice-cold lake water or because of my streak of passion. The rain was now plummeting heavily on our cottage roof and the sound of lightning thundering as it knocked over a tree brought my dazed aunt back to her senses. I had never spoken to her like this before and we both knew it and felt sheepish.

Brie quietly gave me a towel and a cup of warm cocoa, sat me down on the couch and folded her arms plaintively saying, "You're right Esme, you deserve to know the truth, you're old enough so I think it's time for me to tell you the entire story". She sighed heavily, shutting her eyes and shaking her head to brush off all the hardship she was going to have to tell me the truth. I looked at her expectantly and crossed my legs to comfortably hear what she had to say. I already knew this would be a long night. "Five years ago, after I graduated college and was on a cooking camp tour with my friends and we were creating the best survival cooking food using ingredients found out in the wild. I was exploring the moors of the campgrounds we inhabited to look for food and I heard strange whirring sounds, obviously, I decided to intervene because, like you Esme, I was a curious girl who liked to poke her nose in eldritch things". She looked at me patronizingly and I responded with a sardonic half-smile. What I loved most about Brie was that she spoke to me like I was a mature adult but also kept her protective strong spirit shielding me from any dangers outside our little fairy tale cottage.

"I told my friends to explore ahead without me as I would catch up with them later on and I followed the sound with my keen hearing", she continued. "I walked on for miles and miles, and my curiosity was getting the better of me, I was far away from the camping fields and I suddenly remembered that I was dehydrated and starving so I ran to a thick clump of trees where I saw a glimmering, opaque covered ring in the middle of nowhere. I walked into it and I felt myself get thrown onto a hardwood floor which was shaking obstreperously like it knew it contained an intruder. I was too weak to run now and just wanted food and water but with all my leftover curiosity, I crouched underneath a huge antediluvian table where I heard noises from."

"What happened then Aunt Brie?", I asked her, completely hooked on her story although I still didn't understand how this concerned the equivocal antics she did to 'protect' me. As if reading my expression Brie conspicuously remarked, "I saw a little girl running across what seemed like a dark hallway in front of me with flickering lights, she must have been a ripe age of eleven with the most piercing cerulean purple eyes I had seen before. Her jet-black hair seemed intact but the rest of her was tattered and torn. There were bruises covering her from head to toe! It was like seeing a human surviving a vampire attack and I was shocked beyond grief to see such a sight".

"There were screams, belt swinging and threats of murder heard from the next room and I hugged my knees hoping they wouldn't find me but I knew what was going on just then..." Brie blinked back tears and gave the floor a look of such pure consternation as I saw her swallow hard as if the grotesque remembrance of her young years made her want to sink into the floor as it swallowed her. "What happened next?", I urged her to continue. "The girl saw me and ran to me, she looked so happy to see me that without knowing who I was, she embraced me with an endearing hug and a crystal glass of water that appeared out of nowhere. I asked her where she got it from after thanking her and she put a finger to her lips and brought out more water from a nearby table and dipping her fingers into it magicked up a swirl of bright light that she placed into my palm and closed it herself telling me to keep it. She then declared that I should leave immediately or I would be hurt too and with her frantic help, I tried to get out of the house into a very gloomy street. I learned that she couldn't leave because of the door recognising her body's DNA wouldn't permit it. I waved goodbye and as soon as I did, I saw the screams I heard earlier belonging to a middle-aged couple who struck her with their whips immediately because they heard voices. That poor child was being abused and her magical powers itself couldn't save her and I felt ever so helpless after that".

Brie glanced at me just then and quipped, "I was so horrified at what I had just seen that I went to the nearest police I could find and they came along and tried to take the child away from her home to save her and arrest those people but it was a mistake, The people who lived near the house were belligerent and very cruel and fully supported the abuse the poor girl faced so they tried to capture the child as she was being rescued and in the spirit of that struggle, somebody threw some water on the girl and she burst and exploded causing beads of radiated light to unfurl everywhere, it was all over the news for two years after that". "What happened when she exploded?", I asked with bated breath, I felt terribly sorry for that girl but she sounded too good to be true. "She wiped out the entire city", Brie said placing her hand on mine. "The girl had powers whose source was never detected by any scientist in History but her powers did things according to her emotions. When she was happy and gave me the ball of light, it didn't harm me because I was an ally she saw as she had never seen a stranger before. When all those city folk tried to capture her and incarcerate her, she was terrified and angry at them so she exploded causing a rampage of murder but I survived because she knew I was there to help her. When other people got to know about the incident, they saw the girl as a monster and wanted to do away with her but I couldn't let them harm her because she was innocent so I tried to sneak her away to a place where nobody would harm her but her powers couldn't be concealed and in the end, I brought her to Abilo where a good friend of mine called Kingsley stayed in, he agreed to keep her us in the town safe and sound, cut off from the rest of the world as long as she didn't harm anyone because her powers would only grow stronger with age so he used a memory wiping serum on her so that the girl wouldn't attest to be a liability anymore and it was better for her to start afresh as a normal child who never knew she had powers and all I had to do was keep away from large water bodies".

There was a sharp pang of realization dawning on me as I discerned the girl to be me. My head was bursting with questions. Was I that monster who wiped away a whole city? No wonder Aunt Brie wanted to keep me sheltered and was so overprotective. "How come I can shower and drink water than without killing anyone?", I inquired tentatively. The latter smiled saying, "The memory serum wiped out any overindulgence of emotion and the water you regularly use doesn't have strong enough molecules to revive your memory or powers but water stores memory so a larger quantity of it would not only give you parts of your memory back but would also return your powers because that little girl was you my dear Esmerliah but believe me, you are not dangerous and it wasn't your fault". "Wow, that's a lot to digest", I said. "Take your time Esme", Aunt Brie said hugging me understandingly. "Remember, I love you ever so much, it's been five years since I found you and I can't imagine loving somebody more than I adore you". She left the room to get her glasses after that. Her affection may be pure for me but I was conflicted about my own character, I was not who I thought I was…

CHAPTER 3

The Lake's Light

I was hassled over what stung the most, being the freak who murdered an entire city with some light source spurting out of her or the fact that my childhood had faced considerable trauma of being abused through lacerated memories so blemished that it had to be wiped out using a powerful memory serum. I tossed and turned in bed all night long, sleep became a stubborn longing I desired but every time I shut my eyes, my head would fill with thoughts of Brie's story, drowning me in paroxysms of my anxious perception of my reality. I had always thought I was a normal girl living in a normal town of strange people with an appreciation for my surroundings but I was wrong. Abilo was forced to house me out of its kindness but they never could truly accept me as they knew me for who I was… Everybody knew me except for me and that put things into a different perspective.

"Who am I?", I muttered out loud. No matter what my aunt says, I sounded deathly and I couldn't forgive myself unless I knew what I was thinking of that very moment the accident happened. Good people don't spare themselves any mercy if they understand themselves to be notably wrong, besides I was inquisitive to see what my past looked like to fill the gaping hole in my head that erased my past self. The only troubling occurrence was how I would be able to satisfy all these requirements. A flickering light outside my window brought me this answer. "The lake!", I thought excitedly. I had completely forgotten my encounter with the horse and my delicious dip in the cool water. That must have been why there was a shimmer of light when I passed my hand over it. I ripped off my bed covers, packed a tiny overnight bag of clothes and necessities, and padded downstairs cautiously tossing some leftovers my aunt kept in her larder. I quickly scribbled a note and placed it on the table informing my aunt what I was about to do hoping she would understand and not worry about me too much but I was determined to find out who I was.

I left using the backdoor as I was sensible enough to realise that there would be somebody patrolling the lawns outside my cottage to stop me from going on any night adventures as a precaution. "Silly of them not to guard the backdoor, oafs!", I thought savagely as I saw a man from the distance, dressed in black bulkily standing outside almost nodding off to sleep. I wondered how many times Brie or Inspector Kingsley assigned a man to guard a door, I never noticed before at least.

I carefully made my way across the streets trying to stay in the shadow of the trees to avoid being seen, flashing my torch occasionally to see where I was going. "It's like a maze in the dark, I'm never finding it", I grumbled as I missed the right turning to the dark alleyway twice. Thinking back on this experience, I would probably have searched for a different water body but this was the most discreet and magical one. All of a sudden, I heard a large crunch of a leaf and I gasped covering my mouth hoping against hope I wasn't going to get caught again. Luckily, it wasn't a human... A slow whinny made me turn around to see the horse I had helped before and I stroked her mane gently delighted to see her again. "Hello again! What are you doing here all by yourself?", I asked her as she cheerfully nuzzled against my shoulder passing a warm feeling over my body that shouldered my disquietude. "Do you have a name?", asked her and she just stared dolefully at me reminding me very much of a Greek Pegasus with alluring eyes. "I think I'll call you Ambrosia after the Greek balm of immortality", I told her bowing down. I had always been enticed by tales of Greek mythology, gobbling down the antics of Apollo or the wisdom Athena would leave with the other gods of Olympus.

Ambrosia seemed to like the name and after receiving her permission, I mounted her back and continued my journey to the lake. Ambrosia seemed to know the way better than I did so I let her lead the way while I got accustomed to the regular patterned sound of her hooves clomping against the rough ground. The salty night breeze of the trees made my long dark hair flow behind me as well as Ambrosia's mane, it was like a fairy-tale and I guffawed in joy as we arrived at the lake. The moonlight glow made it shimmer like a thousand diamonds spread across a wealthy person's bed and I breathed in the fresh air quenching it in as if it was my last breath. I was anxious about what the water would do to me. "Okay Ambrosia, this is the moment of truth", I announced and Ambrosia patiently waited as I kneeled beside the lake and without thinking passed my hand through the water. Nothing happened and I immediately retracted it.

I sighed, the suspense was sending pangs of worry down my throat and my adrenaline was rising but I tried again letting my hand float in the water for a few seconds but nothing happened. Ambrosia pawed the ground and shook her head violently. "You're a genius Ambrosia!", I exclaimed. "Last time I did jump into the water and if water does revive memories, then maybe it needs my full body to enter it", I quipped and quickly stripped and lowered myself into the water shivering a little. I kicked my legs a few times and waved my hand about, but there was no sight of any light emerging from me. I took a deep breath and grabbed handfuls of water just like I did before and I squealed as I saw a bright light surrounding me like a circle, slowly spreading around the water like an upside-down halo.

"Oh my god, this is incredible!", I cried as I made swirls of light swivel around me and bounce in tiny dancing sticks before disappearing into thin air. Ambrosia looked astounded. For a spare moment, I didn't remember how minacious this same magic was five years ago because I was having too much fun playing around with it. "Here Ambrosia, I'll make you a tiara", I said happily and I closed my eyes visualizing a sparkling golden tiara with blue and white flowers on it and moved my fingers around in the water imagining I was creating it when I opened my eyes, lo and behold. The most enchanting tiara I had ever seen, its fine golden colour resembled the wealth of a thousand kings, the flowers looked so mystical and shimmery, it felt like I could have touched it and it would disappear, its water magic guarding its stability, powerful and overwhelming. I neatly made the tiara land between Ambrosia's ears and she seemed ever so pleased to be wearing it. I had always had a lucid imagination; I had always been able to control my dreams when I was asleep and picture all my senses through just my subliminal mind so it made sense that I could magic up things with light in the water. I didn't find it esoteric to visualize what I wanted and it was very facile for me suddenly. I played about a bit more and then I heard the obnoxious sound of a truck's wheels close by. "Why is there always somebody nearby when I come here", I groaned but didn't get out of the water.

How could I when I just found out that I had water powers if that's what it could be called? A distant voice which I distinguished to say 'Abilo adoption agency' startled me and made the light around me spin like multiple tornados. "Oh dear, they're here to check up on me like Brie said yet I never knew why they were coming and I doubt she knows either", I told Ambrosia panicking and coming to my senses when she started whinnying in alarm. I looked at myself and yelped. "Oh dear, it's the emotions I feel, the magic goes crazy like it happened when I was eleven", I realized. "I should probably get out of the water now". I tried to get out but the light was almost Herculean. The flashing tornadoes spun around faster mingled with my emotion of panic as it bound tiny strings of light together clasping my hands like a prisoner's." Oh dear!", I said acknowledging the severity of the mistake I made. My panic rose at this thought but that didn't ease the light and instead made it go haywire as it rose and started engulfing the entire alleyway like a magical monster. I was helpless and yet I couldn't control it because I wasn't as strong as my magic was. The light tornadoes spun around me like a spinning top making me dizzy and probably delusional as I could have sworn, I saw a roughish face peer at me from the light and say, "Aren't you a tad bit ditzy?" in a heavy southern accent.

"Who are you and please help me, I can't control it!", I half yelled, half sobbed. The face that appeared once every time the tornadoes spun at a three-sixty-degree angle loudly spoke, "Jump into the water holding your breath and wish to escape the place you're at missy". I nodded nervously and followed her instructions trying my hardest to visualise my escape even though I felt weak by the force of my own magic and worried about what it would do. "Try harder girlie, you're as weak as my knees used to be sometimes", the face said. I couldn't see her mouth much at all so I assumed it was a face talking to me although I can't help wishing this was all a bizarre dream although I doubt it because if it was, I would know. I took a deep breath and sank underwater again visualizing with so much concentration that it was odd my eyes didn't pop out of their sockets and float up with the light. It must have worked because I felt a peculiar swooshing sensation as my body lifted upwards writhing in pain and was tossed up and down by an invisible force until it came to rest which I couldn't feel as I passed out midway right after belching yesterday's dinner all over the space around me.

CHAPTER 4

Betty Harbour the Fugitive

I have no recollection of what stirred me awake or any incandescence I was supposed to feel that made my magic attain a higher power over me and all I did remember was this horrid feeling of panic that seemed to rise a thousand feet up in the sky and make me feel like I was in the middle of a horrid nightmare. The last thing my eyes were open to see were the scintillating flares of a silver mist bubble that now held my limp body like a cradle. I opened my eyes sharply and blinked several times. There was nothing around me except for the bubble I was in and the rest of the world looked like a maze of shambolic colours filtered with bright light and floating green leaves. There were mesmerizing shades of colours around the bubble much like a broken television screen but colourful and less strained on the eyes. Bright ochre yellow and fuchsia pink covered the top and bottom part of the translucent bubble with sharp strokes of sky blue and sea green swimming into the former colours. What was really mesmerizing about the whole thing was that it slowly moved to and fro like it was alive, the colours would converge and diverge like a Michelangelo painting in the making and its brilliance was excitable and very extraordinary.

A looming face jumped out at me interrupting my wonder and yelling, "HALLO GIRLIE!". It was the same face that had helped me escape Abilo when my magic turned into pure chaos. Did it freak me out that a face from a lake was telling me what to do? A little bit but I did also hear my aunt's story of me being a monster and saw how that could have happened by disobeying every rule she ever gave me so I digressed and greeted my companion saying, "Hi Lake face, care to tell me what's going on and why I'm sitting in a bubble with just colours around me?". The face guffawed merrily and introduced herself, "Of course, ya would like to know, I'm Betty by the way. Betty Harbour… I saw some trouble in the classified side of the waters and I decided to investigate with my love for danger". The merry twinkle in her eyes despite her being just a face camouflaging with the colours around me astonished my dignity of being a vulnerable human for as long as I could remember.

"Betty, I'm Esmerliah, I don't know my last name but I went into the water even though I didn't fully comprehend what these could do", I said holding up my hands as glowing shimmers of light escaped my palms peacefully. "Are you always just a face?", I asked her curiously as she stared at me unblinkingly for a while making me uneasy. "Umm, Betty?" She blinked then quipped, "Sorry I was trying to see if it would freak ya out and it did", she announced cheerfully. "Oh no, I do have a body but it's just easier to travel around being a substance of water but I'll show myself to you". She stepped forward and her face bobbed up and down like a bobblehead and a head of flaming red hair and piercing purple eyes. She had naturally raised eyebrows and a figure so slender and dainty that she felt fragile although the glow she radiated told me that she had high levels of power that shielded her beauty which bore no recognition in the world outside the water because she was rather an unusual being given her appearance and her ability to be a camouflaging head.

Betty floated in front of my bubble and popped it with her fingernail holding my arm with one hand steadily so I don't fall. "How do you just float and where are we?", I questioned and she smirked saying, "You're magic, you just do and we are currently at everything". She let go of me and to my bemusement, I floated without falling although I found her statement to be baffling and a million questions flooded me once more. "What do you mean Betty? And what do I do about Abilo, I hope my magic didn't hurt anyone", I asked scared. "Who are you anyway?". "Aren't ya a demanding little girlie Esmerliah", she replied. "I'll answer your questions though because I want to, I'm a fugitive who after no money for years trained to be a criminal at the Harbour Federation and we would go from one house to another and kill people for their money and sometimes took their children hostages. Good days", she said wistfully and chuckled at my look of horror. Betty launched herself higher in the space we were in and I was now convinced we were still in the water. "Don't ya worry about me killing you, you're not mortal and your little home is fine since you left pretty quick. Anyway back to me, the federation was successful for years until it got new heads who didn't appreciate people like me making too much money so they kidnapped me and after I tried to kill them, they forced me a pill that made my insides burn and I became this, I live in the water now… I have absolutely no idea how and why but here I am until I saw you the damsel in distress"

"Woah, I think I have been overwhelmed at least three times in the past twenty-four hours and I'm assuming this is a place where people like you and I live in", I said looking around. "it's my favourite place in all waters, you can do everything here and see everything", Betty said changing herself into a scarlet tennis ball and back to herself. "So, you're a shapeshifter?", I inquired and she shrugged. "I can see everything happening in the water too, but I'm still a fugitive and the federation has probably hunted me down for years after all the people I killed especially after the rampage I went on without their notice when I killed people as a sport". Her tendency of casually confessing criminal activity without a shred of remorse didn't cease to frighten me. "What are you then?", she asked me abruptly folding her legs and floating flat on her stomach. I sighed and told her my story and everything about the lake, Ambrosia and Aunt Brie's revelation. "You know the rest", I concluded and she nodded staidly. "Wait, the town that got completely wiped out of its population wouldn't happen to be Kipsy City, would it? The one next to Texas?" Betty asked me. "I don't know, my memory was wiped out and I still can't seem to remember things even though I have my magic back, why would it matter anyway?", I responded. "Esmerliah, that's the city I grew up in right before I moved to murder humans, it was a weird place though and had very odd rules and people, I had an exceedingly difficult escape trying not to be caught and kept as a prisoner in my hometown", Betty mentioned. "Anyway, if what you told me is true and you want to find out what you don't remember then I propose an adventure", she said her eyes gleaming with mischief that I should have known not to trust but I was equally desperate.

"Alright then, take me to Kipsy City and help me find out about my past", I said at last. "Brilliant, we'll be travelling through this water in the place you imagine as your old home, can you do that?", Betty asked and I took deep breaths, spinning my fingers around to transport myself with Betty. "I don't want to hurt anybody else and I might be too dangerous for you if I lose control again". Betty glared at me replying, "Woah, me being a criminal doesn't convince ya does it? I'm magic so you can't hurt me and don't worry you're with me, I won't let you hurt anybody else even if it's fun", she groaned and I shot her a dirty look making her laugh again. Betty had a very infectious laugh which was starting to grow on me. "You don't have a last name either", I realised out loud. "You just took it from that federation. "Girlie, you're a good one for stating the obvious, now swivel ya hands together and take us to Kipsy City, I'll guide you", said my new companion and I did as I was told, bringing my hands together and imagining what my homeland was, Betty seemed to be helping because the magic felt less heavy and more guided, in control which was how I liked to be. A soaring sensation made me shut my eyes tight as I felt the light surround Betty and me taking us to a different place... I really hoped this was a good idea.

CHAPTER 5

Playback on Kipsy City

"We're here Esme!", Betty announced as I felt my feet stand up automatically. I opened my eyes absorbing the mendaciously silent scenery of Kipsy City, the location of our arrival and the apparent home of our robbed childhoods that I was facing again for help and answers to who I was. It was quite like how Aunt Brie described it, a normal magical looking land with trees and bushes everywhere but there was something decidedly amiss about the place, its truth seemed to be concealed and protected in a hidden safe, too defensive to reveal its honesty and the air was dead much like the people were after my past self was done with them yet I was intrusive enough to ignore the deathliness of the place with the help of a convict who's hilarity depended on her abrasive nature and immortality.

Betty stepped out of the water, her thin and wiry body steadfastly walking across the muddy woods as she spun around breathing in the air. "Come out of the water!", she hollered and I obeyed brusquely trying to let go of all my emotions so my magic wouldn't get the better of me for the third time. We walked ahead, our feet trudging across the leaf -scattered ground, the constant snapping of twigs being the only lively noise we could hear in a mile. "There aren't any tourists here, are they?" I asked Betty and she shook her head saying, "There are the occasional brave crowds of people or the mortals who want to hear about the story of the girl but not a lot of inhabitants in this whole place, they're too afraid of magic and fear having the same fate as the people before". "Makes you question your own strength doesn't it, you never know who you could harm", I said sardonically. We walked for a few more minutes and then came across a clearing with no trees but a gigantic waterfall that fell onto a river furiously, it was fascinating to look at but didn't seem to serve any purpose. "That waterfall is our entrance to the city, it's the portal for us to enter and create chaos or have the occasional laugh at times", Betty informed me stretching out a hand into the waterfall and I could see her fingers turning into shapes of hexagons and triangles as she spun her wrist. "Come on Esme, just walk through it". I stepped into the waterfall feeling another large clear bubble surround me and I kept moving forward giggling in delusional shock, it wasn't every day you see a bubble shield you from getting drowned while walking to a different town, Betty's head swam beside me as a part of the waterfall and by now I was accustomed to seeing her new shapes.

The waterfall ended just then and an entire city of tall buildings and houses loomed before I kept my hands in my jumper's pockets just to be safe. "Well here we are, Kipsy City", Betty said displaying the area to me with her outstretched arms. Kipsy City appeared like it had been mangled, the pungent scent of rotting food kept over time and cesspits to bury the dead people made my mouth feel heinously bitter. Everything was crumbling around us, the material of the buildings looked tarnished and weary, the trees looked dead and there was not a soul to be spotted walking around. Betty led me to a little post office and started ransacking the place, opening locks and pulling drawers open to check their mail. "How does this help me regain my memories?", I inquired and stopped talking when a human figure walked into the room crossly. "Who are you and what do you want? I have no time for little busybodies so get out before I report you", he scolded. He was a postman or a caretaker of some kind with bushy eyebrows and a tiny little moustache that looked comical.

"Who are you, do you look after this place?" I asked him politely but his temper wasn't in the mood for chivalry. "Tourist, are you? Always interfering in our business, Kipsy City is closed for people mind you, now go off to wherever you came from", he growled. "Now ya listen", Betty began. "We are not tourists, in fact, we are from this place so we're not going to listen to ya puny little tantrums", she continued, pointing her long fingernail under the caretaker's chin as a threat. "I will call the police", the caretaker responded angrily and Betty spat at his face unnecessarily. "Do ya even know who we are? I'm Betty Harbour for your information and this is my new friend Esmerliah". Our names seemed to hold great power equivalent to our water magic because the vexed caretaker transformed suddenly into a trembling, eager-to-please man, pleading for our mercy. "Please don't hurt me, B-B-Betty? The woman who killed my old colleagues, everyone thought you were dead when we couldn't catch you and Esmerliah, the girl who murdered everyone in this city? How are you two here and what do you want?". I felt bad for the poor man who probably didn't get paid as much as he should for taking care of a city as cursed as this one so he did deserve an explanation even if I didn't have all my facts straight.

"It's alright Mr. Caretaker, we aren't here to hurt you and what happened all those years ago was a grave mistake, you see my memories were wiped ever since then so I came here with Betty to get answers about my past from what I know, if you help us, you'll be doing the city a good deed", I said diplomatically launching into the whole story about me again. "We're trying to make things right, please". The latter nodded amending my comprehension of his name stating, "Alright I'll help you and you can call me Felis".

There was no possible way to find the house Brie had told me about and Betty didn't seem to know much about them either so my old parents had probably been really strong and dangerous folk since Betty was a professional, however, Felis turned out to be more than just a regular caretaker and gave us exemplary assistance on our adventure by using technology that I had never seen before to search for my house. "This is a DNA Housing Tracker, since you were still in the city five years ago, it will be able to track your old location and tell us where you lived", Felis said holding out a syringe connected to a large green, translucent tube with wheel and wires visible inside. "Won't it get muddled up with places she has visited before?", Betty asked smacking her gum loudly which she had found in a drawer nearby. It was repulsive but she didn't seem to be concerned and the decaying gum that was half-covered with fungus seemed to bear no disgust from her but then again, Betty was rather an unpredictable person but you couldn't help getting fond of her.

"Well, no madame, every house in this city had their DNA samples attached to their houses which would last for seven years before being reset to newly collected DNA samples in case somebody had to change their houses after seven years and that's how nobody left the city at the time… well until the attack at least", Felis mumbled awkwardly. "Wait why couldn't anybody leave?", I asked Felis as he inserted the syringe needle into me making me wince for a second before clicking some keys on a tiny computer attached to the DNA Housing Tracker's tube. "There was an agency called the Harbours or something and they asserted dominance by not letting anybody escape with their vile dark forces that nobody really knew about", he postulated. Betty nodded at this; she had been a part of this agency until her free spirit turned her into a fugitive in unforgettable circumstances.

"Okay, I think I have your house", Felis said as a large beep determined our destination and made the eager caretaker's eyes bulge. "The Hallows…" His voice trailed off and Betty jumped up the table and parked herself down cross-legged ushing Felis aside to read the screen. Her flabbergasted face made her drop the nasty chewing gum and give me a pointed look. "You were abused and trapped by the Hallows", she remarked bitterly. "Esme, they were the new heads of the Harbour federation who made me take the pill, they were horrid people and so powerful, everybody listened to them". My eye twitched but I was insistent on finding out more. "Please take me to the old house, I still need answers", I said plaintively and Felis ushered me outside the post office leading Betty and me down the street to a large tower settled on top of a penthouse, its perfectly balanced infrastructure was extraordinary. Felis knew a way in so we entered through the front door and there lay the house I had the unhappiest times in before my memories were wiped. The oak and wooden floors taunted my innocence, inviting me to a world of darkness and despondency. Betty also realised this because she placed her hand on my arm saying, "Ya don't have to do this girlie, we can find another way, don't want to be messing with bad people".

I explored the house and found the circular staircase that led to the top of the tower where I assumed I had been trapped. I found the ring area, Brie had entered the house from and the tall antediluvian mantelpiece where a jug of filled water was still standing, I was certain that if I did remember anything, this would look exactly the same so I ventured closer to the mantelpiece examining the jug of water. Felis had settled down on a nearby chair in front of the large wall tapestry resembling a large wolf preying on people. "Well, do you remember anything?", he demanded his arms folded, he seemed extremely uncomfortable being in this all to powerful house and I couldn't blame him although his bravery and help were much valued.

"Not yet", I answered suspiring the foul air of the house about to give up searching for even a faint trace of recollection when a brainwave hit me." Wait!", I squealed. Brie's story accounted for me dipping my bruised fingers into the glass of water and creating a souvenir for her and if water did retain memory, then I would remember something if I replicated the incident. "Give me a knife and cut my hand a little, I need a cut or a bruise", I told Betty who looked at me as if I was unhinged. "Come on Betty, I know how to remember but I need you to cut me, you're the best person to do it quickly", I urged anxiously until she agreed and used a pocketknife to slash a slightly deep cut into the soft area of my palm. My excitement surpassed the pain it caused me and the quick movements made it easier as I cleaned up the blood quickly and dipped my hand into the glass of water concentrating on my wish to remember. "Nice water replication Esme, that may succeed", Betty encouraged and I felt the water in the glass ripple as a little as a bright swirl of light began to form like the story. I pulled it out and made it disappear into thin air by snapping my fingers, I was getting used to visualization being partnered with my magic at this rate. "Did it work?", Felis asked inquisitively and I just shrugged. Momentarily, more light started to bubble in the tiny glass of water and started expanding swallowing the three of us in its brightly lit embrace.

"I think it's working alright caretaker, can't wait to see how this turns out", Betty said, the bubble of light getting smaller and squishing us together. "I'm scared", Felix said as Betty laughed lightly enjoying the whole scene. The moment of truth was arriving but was I ready to face its swindled gaiety and extinguished yet horrifying memories? Well, we would just have to find out…

CHAPTER 6

The Tunnel of Memories

The bubble was now flashing with visually moving pictures of people I could faintly recall interacting with, the sounds of their voices rang aloud in the bubble loud and clear, its memories a little too vivid for a recorded playback. “Esmerliah, please verify it’s you opening the tunnel of lost memories and not anybody else”, a cool female voice said. Felis and Betty retreated nodding at me encouragingly. “Ya go find out what ya need to Esme, we’ll wait for you here and comfort you if ya need it”, Betty declared and she and Felis stepped out of the bubble. “It’s only me”, I said and the bubble stopped moving in response. I touched the moving picture of a furious woman & a wizened old man and was propelled into it, the pictures now taking the form of live versions of people who were alive and breathing next to me.

“Hello, where am I?”, I asked the woman who didn’t respond but my background told me that it looked like an earlier version of the federation Head’s house in Kipsy city where I was trapped for several years. The woman completely ignored my attempts to get her attention and instead turned to the wizened man brutally saying, “It’s time for the physical since she got away the last time, feel free to use your hands too for the whipping”. The last part was an added whisper but it startled me all the same. I could see a young slip of a girl, the mere age of nine or ten tiptoes at the corner of the room, she had dark hair with some strands of blue with glowing purple eyes, they were mesmerizing and she held some sort of familiarity about her although I had never seen her before but what happened next made me understand who she was. "Run child", I warned the little girl but she too pretended as if I wasn't there.

"There she is", the beastly woman said agonisingly. "Get her Gregnich". The man gave a thin-lipped smile as he brought out a belt and slapped the girl across her face with it creating a red mark across her jaw. I gasped in shock realising that the young girl no other than me years ago was the one getting belted by the nefarious old man. "Stop!", I wailed as the child tried to dodge the whips screaming in pure anguish. Gregnich whipped her several times getting both her arms and legs as illustrated by the sharp new slashes of red-hot blood that dripped down her body. What astounded me was the pain tolerance the child had, she tried her best to get the whip or run away but the man kept pulling her back to hit her whilst his wife stood there, whooping and cheering whenever a new cut was made on the girl's body.

I could only stand there and watch terrorized, that was me getting abused and goodness knew how many times that happened because I didn't seem to be bemused or new to what was happening. Every time I tried to grab the whip, my hand would just float through it which meant I was just a viewer and couldn't do anything about the ongoing scene. It was like watching a horror movie and when you try to tell the protagonist not to go into any dark places where it's terribly obvious the predator was waiting for its victim but of course, they don't listen.

The man promptly threw the whip away and pressed his fingers against the child's neck tightly making her gasp for air as he lifted her right off the ground and punched her oppressively in the stomach five times. The girl who looked starved anyhow looked as if she was about to pass out and never woke up. My blood was boiling, my insides writhing with mortification as I watched in terror as she used her right foot to kick the man in front of her but the slight yet courageous venture of reprisal didn't cause too much of a blow for the criminal-minded man and instead surged his pejorative counterpart who held the poor girl's legs together as the man grabbed her and flung her across the room where she landed heavily on top of a glass table, making it shatter into a thousand pieces.

It's bad enough tripping on a loose glass piece anywhere you go but this might have killed the child as her foot had sunk into so many glass wedges that the blood was just a constant liquid everywhere. The expensive bowl of hydrangeas had also shattered spilling flowers and water everywhere which is when it hit me. I was going to use my water powers in this memory, the child would be safer. As I predicted, the little girl's hands that were now wet sparkled with light as a shield erupted in front of her making the Gregnich fall flat on his ghastly face when he tried to get to her again. The instantaneous fear in the child's eyes was noteworthy but its effects on her magic was even more perceptible. Her undernourished body was now a flaming stick of comeback as he brought down her shield bringing down the huge tube light on the ceiling falling on Gregnich's face knocking him unconscious.

"For that you sleazy girl, you will get no food or water for three days and will never see anybody ever again for the rest of your life, you are to be locked in the tower forever", the woman roared throwing a piece of glass at the child's face who dodged it, her reflexes kicking in. "Please Mamma, you haven't given me food for three days and I have had to find scraps", the high-pitched voice of the child echoed feebly. "No you little beggar, go into the streets and beg for more, oh wait how can you when you are to be locked here forever, looks like you're just going to meet your destiny of death instead", the woman snarled. "By the way, I am not your mother you fool, you're a dirty orphan from the streets". She added and walked away dragging the little child up the long spiral staircase into the plausible tower but I was unable to follow them for the scene shifted to another memory.

This time, the scene was not at the Hallow's house but instead was at a lakeside somewhere in the city that reminded me of the dried-up lake we had seen before when we entered the run-down place. Two police officials were scooping up water in their palms, examining and sniffing it as if water were a frivolous benefit being gifted to them which they had never had before. "It is impossible for the child to change the state of this liquid into different things throughout, she may pose a danger to Kipsy ", the first official remarked scribbling something down in a frenzy. "Madame Hallow had her DNA tracked and taped in their house so she can't escape the tower, I doubt she can do anything now", his accomplice replied.

Child Esme was crouching behind a dark corner of the lake evidently eavesdropping and I really hoped she wouldn't be caught. "How is she. I mean how am I there if I am trapped in the Hallow tower?", I inquired and was answered almost immediately with the sounds of police sirens and sharp voices. "Escapes are happening everywhere, sound the alarm for everybody to stay inside their homes and not come out, the Harbour federation has fallen, assassins on the loose, I repeat the Harbour federation has fallen", a voice announced on a loudspeaker.

I walked a few steps forward and could see people scurrying to get to their houses as armed and masked men with rifles shot wildly around hitting a few innocent and unfortunate passers, it looked like a war was going to break out but young Esme seemed very new and exuberant to check this new world out. Her eyes shone mischievously as she dove into the lake and created moving pictures of swans and tiny sparrows dancing in rows positioning them to float over the official's heads.

"Handcuff her and keep her away from the water", the former official yelled as he returned to the lake holding his gun out vehemently. Esme was hauled out by two men and handcuffed as the men took her away in a police car. Several dead bodies just lay on the roads, their eyes glassy and brooding, they knew in the last second of their lives that they were never going to escape the atrocious conventions of the city and their helpless arms crossed at their sides bore the symbol of freedom as they had escaped the Dystopia of Kipsy City. I tried following the young Esme and the officials but like the previous memory, an invisible wall in the middle of the road kept me from ensuing the little party and switched to a new memory, one that stupefied me the most.

I was back in the Hallow's house and Brie's story of the entrance was spotted by me now and her disappearance progressed just as quickly. My aunt looked noticeably young and less worried in this memory, she was always an unbelievably beautiful woman and in the memory's splendour, she radiated high levels of a pulchritudinous allure than usual. "I think we have to let her loose, it's the only way the city will understand how serious the Harbour federation is and the riots will cease effective immediately", Madame Hallow said to Gregnich who was tossing over a knife in his hand, admiring its honed tip. "We have way too many fugitives who didn't react well to the serum, the DNA sequencing must have been meddled with due to human errors and once we find out which lab rat did that, they will obviously be executed but we need to unleash the monster Kipsy doesn't expect first", she continued earnestly. "Are we aware of how much power she actually holds? I mean we can just destroy her when she turns eighteen so why risk setting her free and away from our plans", Gregnich replied nastily.

"Then we show the people of Kipsy that we have more power by beating her up, get the knife ready because after we're done, we need to get out of this place so while the little skank is getting abused here turning everybody's attention towards her, we need to get out and look for the right serum for our fugitives because I am certain, that two-timing double crosser Betty isn't dead, her body wasn't found", Madame Hallow said growling and her partner gave an iniquitous laugh saying, "Alright, don't forget to throw the water on the girl, we need her to throw her biggest fit of rage yet if this is to work". The scene shifted to the night; Brie saved the younger version of me which was unplanned. I couldn't see the Hallow's disappearance from the scene so I climbed a tall oak tree in the middle of the city which had a good vantage point over most parts and I found my target sneaking out of the city with zip lines, lightly zig-zagging across the dead bodies who fell with the water magic that was being emptied of the little girl's stomach, preferably to take another high secret portal out of the city like the fountain and the ring. The Hallow's plan may have malfunctioned but they did get away which meant that Brie, Betty and I were not the only ones who made it out of the city alive. The Hallow's had too and they may still be alive plotting for more calamities.

The tunnel of memories switched off its tape and the light bubble around me faded away returning me to the room where Betty and Felis looked at me expectantly awaiting my dire remarks on what I had seen. Some of my memories may have been getting jogged but what I knew I didn't remember and that was something nobody had information about. "I saw the night of disaster where everyone was killed by my defence curse", I said at last after a moment of irrelevant silence. "The Hallow's didn't die that night, the attack was planned, they understood what would ignite for my magic to run haywire and they planned for me to die with the city people even though I didn't thank to Brie". "What does that mean?", Felis asked indefinitely. "It means they were looking for the source of my magic for the serums they gave the Harbour federation criminals and they are probably still alive planning to overthrow more than just one city", I informed them nettled at the thought that the clearance of my memory had only put a lot more people in danger across the world.

CHAPTER 7

Golden Gateway to Another Mystery

"There is a part of me that is so full of anguish that the pain built up within harrows my inner deathliness", I said staring transfixed at the tiled floors I was seated upon in the Hallow's house. It was all coming back, memories of my past rushing into my head like a conveyor belt of baggage, the heaviness of it was overthrowing me off my sedate manner of curiosity that I had until now to see my past. "I really am a monster and the worst part is, it is my fault the Hallow's will ruin more parts of the world and Abilo and my aunt are in peril too", I said sinking my head into my palms despondently. Betty patted my head maternally saying, "Esme it isn't your fault, you were tormented all your life by the Hallows and their rule was Dystopian by nature, it was sheer luck we all got out when we did" For once in the unsorted pieces of my life that I struggled to put together, I was lost. Natural curiosity wasn't an essential term that drove me to be adventurous and all I wanted to do was to return to a happy place and stay there without moving.

"Well, what now?", I ask Betty and Felis who both seem uncomfortable after being drowned in the forbidden city of the grotesque past thanks to me. I cannot fully explain how I felt right now. What I can however explain is that the stricken memories of not so long ago were daunting to me. Life in Abilo always seemed like an adventure and I had always taken my aunt's care over me for granted wanting to explore and move past the provincial life but now I would kill to return to it. Losing my memory was one thing but all it sparked was inquisitiveness and not pain but now the pain had finally arrived, physical and mental, it was overbearing yet a reminder that my life was not always what it seemed to be.

A rushing sound of vehicles stopped my rumination as I leapt to my feet raising my hands as industrial weapons. "Ya lying scumbag", Betty growled, and it took me a second to realise that she wasn't talking to herself as she grabbed Felis's collar threateningly. "I'm sorry, I did what I had to, there is no way I'm going to be talking to two freaks like you and all your past troubles", said Felis now awry of Betty flashing purple eyes as she screamed some foreign insults at the top of her voice." This bimbo called the cops on us", she muttered furiously and sure enough, men dressed in heavily guarded armour arrived at our doorstep with large kunais and guns. One man took hold of Betty while three other men steadied her, her wiry arms were strong enough to put up quite a fight and after knocking out two of the men, she was handcuffed and grabbed tightly. "You have the right to remain silent", said the policemen as I frantically searched for some water to throw on Betty so she could transform and escape. Felis just stood by grinning making me want to his smirk of his face with one wave of my hand. "Esme run, I'll be fine, and I'll search for some answers, you go ahead and escape and try find the Hallows too and stop them", Betty yelled at me and I listened.

I ran up the stairs but the policemen seemed to have made their mark there too so I rushed to the bathroom and locked myself in it before getting the tap to turn on. Steaming hot water poured from the faucet nearly burning my skin off but I didn't care, my life was at much too high a risk. The policemen banged on the bathroom door, they had foraged a good deal of the house and very vexingly, I could hear the sounds of Felis command the policemen in lace they could look for me. What a traitor! My hands once again accustomed to the water's natural feel, I used it to shun myself out of the room creating slides as I went along and the door finally swung open despite the two bolts. "There she is, get her!", yelled one policeman after my fleeing feet on top of a gigantic moveable slide. My favourite colour must have been golden or perhaps I would imagine myself to be a regal majesty who rose from her falling ashes. Either way, I was flying and it was the best feeling ever. The water in my hands churned my feelings as they burned with power and passion pushing me forward until I reached the spiral staircase in the middle of the room. The police must have called backup because there were now five policemen each facing both my left and right whilst a couch had been pushed towards the back trap me from escaping in that direction.

I was at a loss; policemen were shooting at me wildly from everywhere now and it was only a matter of time before they hit home. I stared forcibly at the spiral staircase ad made up my mind. I was going to go in there and look for another way, despite any memory of being locked up in a tower room of madness that drove me insane because despite all my abstraction, I knew that it had been purely the Hallow's menacing intentions that drove me to crazy town, to begin with. The water was now almost drying up but I couldn't afford to lose my magical abilities just yet because, without that, I would only be a young girl running away from a dozen men with guns so with all the speed I could emanate, I rushed upstairs and after a long flight, I rolled into a room full of very tiny golden objects, flashy to the eyes in near sight yet seemed old and weary like a forgotten casket. There was no way the men would make it here in time however fast they could run because there were loads of stairs so I investigated the room closely.

Neatly laid out golden brushes, their bristles were perfectly straight like they hadn't been touched in years. Their edges glistened and beamed with golden light much like the golden chains laid out on a mannequin neck with several golden tiaras, each had a centre gemstone of choice, some were ruby red, others were emerald green and others were sapphire blue. Each however contained indistinguishable flashes of golden that were hard to miss. What truly caught my eye was the tiny yet prepossessing golden dress laid out at the corner of the room lying spread-eagled across a mahogany trunk, its seams ran down the dress as golden shimmers of light, and its bodice was tight and absorbing and looked like it would neatly fit the wearer and make them look spectacularly monachal. I ran my finger down the hemline, the chiffon and organdie quality felt light against my caroused fingers from all the weaving of water magic. Suddenly a huge blast of wind interrupted my blatant discovery as I felt my feet sway and fall over and looked around wildly for the cause.

There was nothing around. It was time to go, and I was certain they had taken Betty to the police station already by now, I hope she managed to sly her way out of that one.

Shakespeare must have been right because all the glisters are definitely not gold. After all the more I touched the golden dress, the more wrinkled and disagreeable it became and stopped looking like something I would wear to a royal ball. The tiara's quality too was degrading, and I have no idea why I thought touching every single possession I had was a favourable idea. I spotted a window at the other corner of the room and planned to jump out of it but I had to find water first to conjure up a pillow to cushion my fall and to avoid being on my deathbed even though I believed I deserved it. My heart could not however resist the temptation of touching the mannequin neckpieces wearing necklaces one last time so stroked the necklaces with a farewell gaze before walking towards the window.

The creaking behind me made me turn and see a peculiar thing. The mannequin's head was spinning around! It was a full 360-degree angle and the dress slid onto the floor in a perfect circle, the tiaras landing on a tiny mattress-like bed like an obstacle display. It was the perfect booby trap although I doubted that's what it was. Younger me *had* been trapped inside this tower and I had to flee from all the horrors I saw on a daily basis from the Hallows but this was not a trap but a secret opening!

I peered closely at the opening the mannequins had made as the wall in the tower creaked as it disappeared to the right, the use of some shifting technology being made evident and lo and behold, a slide emerged, like all the objects in the room, it was golden but must have been frequently used because it was a faded lemon yellow now with a wee bit of shine. Curiously, I put one foot on the slide and to the utter diminishment of my general knowledge of a children's playground (Abilo didn't have many entertainments offers for children), it slipped and slid down what was probably the largest slide in the world. "Whoo!", I exclaimed as I slid down the slide in playful fancy until it came to a stop. The slide got over much too soon and I would have been disappointed if it were not for the large cave that stood in front of me. My altitude must have decreased which meant that the cave was underground and peculiarly I could hear a rumbling sound overhead. A large poster on the cave caught my attention, it looked to be done by a younger me with the help of some water magic because the stiffness of the letters was perfected by the golden streaks of my powers.

"Under the sea, you will exploit your true see", read the big, bold, capital letters. This made no sense to me because I neither could see anything under here nor knew what to find when I had only one mission, Find the Hallows, stop their treacherous antics and rescue Abilo at the same time and right now exploring seemed to have gotten the better of me. After all, once again I found myself lost in a new place that would only bring more trouble into my life but it was too late to regret coming here. "Under the sea", I read out again and I looked up realising what the rumbling sound had been. "No way, I'm under the sea", I said incredulously. My voice echoed through the cave entrance and I repeated it, enjoying the sound of my echoed voice beat throughout the cave. What my distracted oblivion failed to question before was how was I under the sea. What place did this cave lead to and what did I do in here before? My memories had most certainly returned but not the minute ones that were well preserved yet too futile to remember.

I cautiously tiptoed inside the dimly lit cave, which was lit up by the tiny little lanterns attached to the cave walls. I walked on ahead until I stumbled across some uneven flooring and the piece of the floor gave away flinging me like a sack of potatoes as I fell for what seemed like 30 minutes but was only a few seconds until I reached solid ground. If the universe planned the lives of every individual creature in the world, mine must have been planned by a drunk person or a person in serious need of some structure because these last few days had been nothing but new adventures, I try to find a connection between these but all I see is a novelty and right now all I wanted was too hit some solid ground-figuratively even though I reached it literally on that note. The daylight was evident in this new place I was in and a young man who looked to be about my age bent over me, picking my hand up. "Esme—Esme, are you okay? I thought you were dead; can you stand?". He was tall, with the softest brown eyes and a handsome smile that curved at the edges. "I think I should take you inside before anyone see you", he told me grimly and he held my arm and dragged me inside the little cottage as I obeyed without a struggle. Who was this boy and how did I know him? Only time would be able to tell and the boy of course, his eyes seemed to glint with attractiveness so perhaps he knew something I didn't. I couldn't tell why but I trusted him and couldn't wait to receive some answers at last!

CHAPTER 8

The Rotating Liah

"Esme, where were you? We all thought you were dead!", the boy now exclaimed enthusiastically and when my seemingly nonplussed look didn't explain his questions, he gently ushered me inside the tiny crumbling cottage. The cottage was an adorable little thing, it seemed to be right out of a fairy tale which was the one beauty for the bracken, tumbled-down area it lay in. It had a roof that radiated a scent of gingerbread, its tiny dress shop windows opened up to reveal its winsome polka-dotted, blue windows that spread the endearing feeling of warmth and frankness. I hurriedly pinned my hair up with a tiny, golden band I had found, stretching it out into a long ponytail behind me as the wind grazed my cheeks, fondling its puffiness from the lack of sleep and worry I had been getting over the past few days. I had lost the grasp of days as a whole and everything just felt like one big dream but now that I was here with this concealed snip of a boy, I felt like my little journey was just bout to get even more uncanny.

"Esme welcome back home!", said the boy kindly as he led me inside the cottage and sat me down on the all too comfortable couch that's seat was like sleeping on the softest clouds as a cloud fairy. I looked out of the window at my right, astounded to see that the view outside contained the most perplexing beauty. There were the leafiest green trees, blundered with happiness as they waved to and fro to the breeze. The several plants surrounding the trees danced and waved copying the tree's motion like a child would often follow an adult's lead. Their leaves sparkled with bright yellow and red flowers, capturing the essence of the most perfect summers day with the finishing touch of a delicious-looking pond with tiny fish swimming about, their mouths blobbing as they swam around in circles, enjoying their habitat of finery even though their memories only lasted about 6 seconds each. I wanted to kick my head back and laugh as I got swayed by the ravishing wind, I wanted to just lie down on the grass that invited me to listen to the birds chirp at the egging-on squeaks of squirrels as they tried to catch the yellow butterflies who very aptly sat on flowers extracting pollen, I wanted to be happy again and this seemed like the most perfect haven.

"You always did love that", The boy remarked buoyantly as he took out a yellow flower and neatly tucked it behind my ear before tearing off one petal. "Why did you do that?", I asked in response and he shrugged. "You always considered flowers to be people, similar to you, one end tattered and fragmented but the others still standing strong and glamourous for everyone to notice its beauty and power no matter what", he responded, his hand sliding down to my shoulder and he patted me contritely. "You should have asked for help Esme, I was your best friend". I felt sorry for him but I couldn't help it. "My memory got wiped after Kipsy City was destroyed", I said absent-mindedly tying a knot with the end of my jumper. "They took me to a safe place where I wouldn't be harmed by the Hallows or killed for what I did, I don't remember everything, I'm sorry so I don't know your name either although you live in the dearest little place". My new ally didn't even turn a hair at this and just patiently introduced himself.

"I'm Levian, your former best friend. You found a gateway to this place from that tower you were trapped in and you would seek refuge at my house, I was a refugee hiding out here after I fled the heart of Kipsy City with my parents but they died fighting the awful federation's control so I started living here by myself until I met you, there is always a new place here whenever you arrive created by the water tanks that I made that you filtered with your magic of mystery after you created the Rotating Liah, it was by far the most impeccable thing your magic has done right before you left… the last time I ever saw you…", his voice trailed off as he blinked really hard and I could tell he was trying hard not to burst into tears in front of me. "That was probably the night my aunt saw me and rescued me, how did my magic grow to that extent?", I inquired. "It was your seventeenth birthday Esme, you were scarred like never before and even though my lifehacks could only help dilate the tremendousness of your bruises, it didn't stop the pain or you looking like a person from war, you were battered down-right before we could celebrate your birthday and when you came to visit me so we could celebrate, you wished you could go to a happy place for some time everyday wherever you wanted and since I had just installed water tanks in this house attached to my backyard, you managed to somehow transform it into a dome of some fantasy land that you would want to go to every time you were upset where we would both hang out that was named after you, we only went to three of the most glorious lands before you had to return to the tower and the entire city died the next day, I have been alone here for years…".

Levian's long speech was rather heartfelt and as my memories would faintly become less blurry each second I concentrated, I was assertive about trusting him, he was quite handy for the young age of 18 and as I looked around distinguishing the different tools he had in his house, I observed the increasingly convoluted drawings of different models that were placed around his house, especially the self-managing kitchen that was currently cooking a pot of chicken broth and meatballs by itself connected to some automatic whirring from a large tablet at the corner of the room that Levian appeared to have programmed for his benefit. The kitchen passed me a glance of a memory where a soaring feeling convulsed my skin passing me the incentive of performing a handstand at the corner against the kitchen table and laughing as I fell. The quiver of a flashback of that exact same moment of a younger Levian laughing at me upside as he caught me to avoid my injurious fall lingered at the corner of my brain. "You're frightfully clever, did you make all of this?", I asked Levian who handed me a plate of chicken broth soup and meatballs that were picked up by a mechanical arm and handed to him. "Yes, I have had some time on my hands, I mean the city never extended to intrude upon my property that I just happen to live in and well I missed you, and so did they", he declared as a brown horse walked up from the Rotating Liah neighing as Levian patted her fondly. "Ambrosia!", I vociferated hugging the horse who no longer wore the headband I had first made using my water magic.

"Wow, you remember her but I over-clogged your brain, didn't I?", Levian demanded sardonically. I laughed and hugged the horse tightly around its neck. "I met Ambrosia in Abilo, she had a thorn stuck in her hoof, I don't know how she's here but...", I stopped talking when I realised something. Abilo never had much of animals, it was rather quizzical that she had been there anyway which explained why the people were super uptight at the mention of the animals. I noticed the tiara; I had made for her earlier was no longer there which made me wonder whether my aunt had found her or not but unfortunately the communication between humans and animals was limited to a bunch of neighs and nuzzles without anybody getting to the point of the conversation.

"Levian, I want to enter the rotating Liah", I demanded turning to Levian pleadingly. If Ambrosia was Levian's pet horse, it meant only one thing, that my magic was strong enough to transport us to places that would make us happy after a long day of torment from my guardians and hiding for Levian's refuge. Levian agreed almost immediately and held my hand gently, guiding me inside the little sunny garden. "Now remember Esme", this may hurt a bit if you see things you don't want to see", he told me gazing at me with a mixture of reluctance and interest for what we were about to see but I was ready. It had been a long while since I knew my life and now, I was prepared to see the horrors it embodied.

I stepped into the Liah, it felt strange but the comfort of Levian's hand made me feel better almost immediately. The spinning began after a three-second pause and my world seemed to rotate round and round, my ears felt green and apparent all of a sudden as I clutched to Levian's hand- the only sense of normalcy I could currently find. He squeezed it and relief flooded me as I took a deep breath. It must have been at least fifteen minutes until the rotating light ceased its spinning and Levian's strong hands nudged me out of the platform and I opened my eyes, a bit hesitantly at first. The world outside looked different from the one I was used to… It had sunshine and flowers just like the little view I could see in the light before I entered it. There was however something else, something different from what felt right. A huge building that read, 'River Valley High' entered my view.

What was this place? I couldn't recall. A large dome-like structure in a medley of flowers sorted out like candy amongst the placid beat of the wind waving about in the arbitrary scenery. 'It's beautiful', I said unsure about the proceedings but Levian seemed alright so I wasn't much worried. 'This must be a memory your magic stored for you after the pool fight', Levian mused as an event of dichotomy prevailed over us with a boy and a girl laughing sporadically. "Who are they?', I asked although my questions were soon to be answered when I was rammed aside by a young, slender teenager with glasses perched upon her dark hair, blue eyes twinkling as she flippantly jumped on the boy's back flinging her things on the floor. 'That's you Esme when you were sixteen, I'm about to show up as well and we're going to see the memory through the characters now', Levian warned me and sure enough, a warming sensation inundated me that ended as I opened my own blue eyes, flipping my dark hair and catching my glasses before they fell to the ground and smashed into a million pieces.

CHAPTER 9

Patrick's Pool Party

It had been a whimsical day, it's not every day you get to sit in an empty classroom and smear cake on one of your closest friend's faces. No matter how altruistic Patrick may pretend to be in front of cute girls, it wasn't in his amalgam of feelings to ever be boring. He may be averse to the idea of a full-fledged party but my friends and I knew he was the most gregarious being to exist and he loved all the fuss. I was sixteen and thriving in many ways, he was turning seventeen so he must have a good party even if it's at school, right? Well not that I had anywhere to go either.

Levian next to me was biting into his share of cheesecake, grinning ludicrously from ear to ear. I smiled, and he seemed happy so why did I constantly feel a sinking feeling in me that all this merriment was about to end? The haplessness I always felt got the better of my judgement but I was determined to have fun on Patrick's birthday.

'Hey, you, okay?', Levian asked me, his eyes searching for any sign of worry and I nodded serving him a bite of more cheesecake. I wasn't okay but now wasn't the time to direct an impetus for a change in the birthday plans. It was perfect, the most affable affair of my friends and I gathered around Patrick celebrating our love for each other on his birthday. Patrick is the all-round player whose previously reclusive mate Grayson has surpassed in picking up girls at parties. Grayson seemed to be enjoying too, his eyes sparkled as he timorously attempted to place a beer bottle on the classroom's whiteboard ledge. Sneaking alcohol into school might have been the boldest thing we ever did.

I think I had a tiny crush on him, he was handsome in many ways with his pristine eyes that glimmered against his upturned nose and rock-cutting jawline. Sometimes all I wanted to do was to draw my hands through his fluffy hair and gaze into his eyes as he held me close to him. "Esme! Look out!", wailed my best friend Olive as she flung an armload of cake in my direction. I ducked and it hit Marshall and Zara in the middle of their faces. After a minute of self-indulgent shock, they fastidiously aimed back at Olive who screamed running across the room and spilling beer everywhere leaving Marshall to immediately try to clean it up. "Guys, don't spill beer, we'll get into trouble", he called out crossly and Olive stopped racing around.

My wonderful friends seemed to have it all figured out as Zara flipped her curly, brown hair and leaned against my shoulder crying in laughter. There they all were, if only I could capture the moment, frozen in memory. I liked all of us together. Marshall, the oldest and most responsible person who took care of all of us and gave the most poignant speeches yet maintained a comical tone every time. Olive, my best friend who was dating Marshall for two years now, was intuitive, deferential to everyone and made us burst into fits of laughter. Levian became steadfast friends with me after I discovered a passageway from my house to his and every time, I was miserable or pained, he was my zenith of clemency for my enervating life. I shuddered at the thought of it and shook my head pushing those thoughts away. I wasn't going to revisit those horrors continuously. I was currently living with Levian while his parents were sick so we were both there for each other a lot and it may have been his liberating intelligence or his sudden addiction to alcohol but he always knew what I wanted and what I felt despite any secrets I concealed. Patrick was everyone's favourite a regular joker who made me constantly burst out laughing at all times of the day. Everyone loved him. And Grayson? He was quixotically attractive, in my eyes at least. He played the guitar quite well and all I wanted was for him to sing to me as I accompanied him.

Zara was like a sister; she was bubbly and sweet yet reserved in some ways. She would never allow a drop of alcohol to touch her lips. Or do anything wild but she was dragged along with the rest of us anyway.

"You know what guys, we should take this party to the pool and rage out there", Patrick exclaimed raising the beer bottle high. His mercurial thought process dragged us to the pool, hiding the bottle and cake in our clothes. I felt the blood rushing through my head as he picked me up and ran outside the school building. Zara piggybacked on Grayson as Levian followed stealing another sip from the bottle. "Levian, don't finish it all here, they'll see us before we reach the pool", Marshall instructed and his prognosis was unfortunately correct as a teacher walked by just then with the Head Boy. "Oh, for heaven's sake", Zara muttered vehemently and glared at the Head Boy while Grayson and Patrick rushed to cover Levian. "What's going on here?", the teacher wanted to know cynically eyeing our little group as the Head Boy tried to examine the room. “Six feet away from my best friend”, Olive called out a little drunkenly as the teacher looked at HB (For the sake of simplification) nonplussed at all the belligerence.

“Okay I’m late for class, so you kids better rush to yours now”, the teacher said and scurried away leaving HB for us. My friends hadn’t forgiven HB for what he had done to me yet. Stalking your ex-girlfriend can get a little out of hand if HB hadn’t been as possessive as he was of me. For a Head Boy, he was rather delusional and it was all thanks to the Hallow’s banishment of me from home when I crashed at River Valley’s boarding where HB also stayed. Dating him might have caused way more regret than I imagined but now that I lived with Levian and was with my friends, there was no way he could besiege me anymore.

“Esme, I need you, you’re not okay and I can help you with that. You are the love of my life; just say the word and I’ll do stuff to make all of these awful people disappear. They’re trying to ruin you”, he said locking eyes with me. “Please don’t bother my friends and me again or I report you for good”, I retorted as Patrick and Zara placated me by rubbing my arm. “Stay away from her or I beat you up, you don’t get to say what’s good for Esme”, Levian yelled and we all walked out of the building from there.

“You really should report him Esme”, Grayson pointed out as we ran to the swimming pool with all our things ready to continue our fun again. “He always gets the better of me when I try”, I shrugged and changed the topic. I had way too much on my plate to worry about HB. The pool looked glorious in all our serendipitous plans. Its clear, shimmering water longingly called us to it as we bathed our legs shivering with 'oohs' and 'aahs' when they hit the liberating element.

"This is life and I am so glad I have all of you here to celebrate my special day with me, I love you all", Patrick announced as we all cheered his joy by taking turns sipping beer from the large bottle. "Oh, come on Zara, it's just one sip", Levian complained as she refused to take even a drop. "You're drinking for two as it is Levian, don't worry about me", she replied. "Okay time to get really wild!", Grayson shrieked as he pushed Zara into the water and she screamed sonorously. "Oh Grayson, I hate you so", she said as the cheeky little Casanova blew a flying kiss out to her. I pushed Grayson in avenging Zara and he indignantly called out to Patrick to fling me in too to which he obliged and Levian trying to save me, plunged in with me.

Marshall disapproving at first joined us after Olive and Patrick too jumped in but after accidentally bumping heads with Olive got out of the pool aggravated. "Marshall gets in", Levian said as he put me on his shoulders as we started wrestling each other with me on Levian's shoulders and Zara on Grayson's.

Patrick suddenly found a random glue bottle that was lying around and everything after that went crazy. The whole poolside was a surfeit of glue, rocks and water and we were bating about fully clothed in a sticky, watery mess. Patrick as usual surprised us all by whipping out another beer bottle and soon the messy mixture had the added component of alcohol as well. Glue streaked in our hair, Zara, Olive and I went to wash up after a while and the guys sat on the steps drinking and Grayson lit a cigarette from his pocket.

I hurriedly locked myself into a bathroom stall as I felt this strange, swelling feeling in me. It had first begun when Patrick pushed me into the pool and it kept growing. The slightly euphoric yet pressing feeling of power coursed through my veins and my fingertips felt a release of power and I gave a little gasp of excitement. "Esme you alright?", Olive called as I walked out. "Yeah, I'm good, it's weird I felt this sensation and I still kind of feel it", I quipped. "Maybe it's love", Zara said smirking, her head tilted sidewards. She was getting all the glue out of her hair. I blushed and she advantageously asked, "Wow, Esmerliah Hallows is blushing but seriously what is going on between you and Levian?". "The same that's going on between you and Grayson Zara, I mean it's obvious Esme and Levian have unresolved feelings for each other but you guys? Spill the beans for Grayson is quite handsome", Olive butted in. I felt a pang of jealousy and repudiation at the same time and I knew it wasn't the sensation but something else stopped me.

"Zara, did you call me Hallows just now?", I asked her quizzically.

"Well yeah, that is your last name isn't it".

"No, I use my Aunt Brie's last name remember?", I replied.

"Esme, I've known you since you were 11, your name is Hallows"

Zara and Olive looked concerned, exchanging glances and Olive held my hand. "Esme, are you sure everything is, okay? I mean I know Mr. and Mrs. Hallows are a bit horrible to you but are you sure you're fine?", she asked but I wasn't fine just then. The power I felt through my hands was electric and the angst of Olive just revealing a secret of mine in front of Zara was becoming unbearable. "I am fine but I can't believe you just said that out loud, I told you that in confidence Olive!", I said angrily and Zara hastily petted me but I was furious. It had been a good day but Olive had to ruin it and the power was growing by the second and I would have to let it out soon.

"Okay I'm just worried about you Esme and I'm sorry but you've had a rough time and maybe you need help". She wasn't making it any better.

"You look a little flushed, maybe we should call the guys and just head back to class", Zara interjected.

"Not everything is about the guy's Zara is what Olive would actually want to say to you because she is burning with envy for you", I said threatened by Olive spilling any secret. I loved Olive, she was the best friend I had ever had but now nothing was going to stop me from attacking her after all the pressure she had put me under that year with her own self-draining problems. Zara looked at Olive confused and I continued to blithely speak in rage. "She is jealous of the attention you get, even the attention I get. Levian, Patrick and Grayson are always closer to us than to her and she loathed Marshall talking to you especially when they've been having fights recently. How about that Olive, what is it like having your best friend turn on you?".

"Girls, is everything okay?", The guys had walked in the washup area after hearing heated voices. "Lovely dulcet tones, what's up?", Marshall asked and put Grayson's cig away after seeing Olive's frown. "Were you smoking Marshall?", she demanded, and he looked lost. "I told you so many times you can't smoke because I don't want to be with a smoker". The realization of my hurtful words earlier must have increased her fury at her boyfriend. "You can't control his every move Olive", Grayson reckoned and gave another cigarette to Marshall. "Watch me, Marshall choose it's the cig or me", Olive argued.

"Guys please don't fight on my birthday", Patrick beseeched but was ignored. The sensation was too strong for me now and I felt like I was about to explode.

"Olive it is my life and after all the sacrifices I have made for you, let me have this one", Marshall said.

"OH, maybe it's because you would prefer to be with Zara"

"OLIVE WHAT IS THE MATTER WITH YOU, WE'VE BEEN TOGETHER TWO YEARS". My head was spinning at all this and Levian was tottering at his heels unable to keep still, the alcohol hitting his senses drastically. This went on for a few minutes until the worst thing happened.

"I'm DONE. Olive, I can't do this anymore, I need a break", Marshall said with a tone of finality in his grave voice.

"Okay fine. We'll continue this later, let's just go back to class", Olive answered. Marshall remained still.

"No. I mean forever; I'm breaking up with you. I need my freedom back and you make me feel pressured all the time. You pressure Esme with your sob stories because you're so dependent on other people. I'm done. Everyone wants to be happy without you ruining it every time even on my best friend's birthday. I don't believe you". With that Marshall began to walk away as Zara cried silently, she hated fights and the tension of this one was too much, Grayson and Patrick looked stoically ahead and just then the power overtook my control.

A huge blast of golden light burst through me and hit the room. Rays of sharp golden daggers panned around the room and figures of faces caterwauling with belts of all sorts. It was much too strong for anyone. A dagger hit Levian knocking him unconscious, Olive hurt her head while the guys and Zara ducked. Everything miserable came back to me and I remembered everything. The Hallow's torment, Aunt Brie rescuing me five years ago, the non-perfected serum they made me drink that made me forget so much. Now I remembered. I remembered going to River Valley and living there again because the Abilo adoption agency adopted me to go back to school so I was made to live in the boarding house. The memory serum had been used for everyone in River Valley High. I was in Kipsy, not Abilo where I belonged. The Kipsy that I had... I... I destroyed.

I was a monster who was living with Levian although I knew I was a menace to everyone, especially him and now I had struck him as I did to the whole of Kipsy. They must have rebuilt the city and there must have been some survivors.

A surge of memories passed through me. Everything was horrid again.

"Esmerliah, it's you who we had to hide from? The water blaster monster?", Marshall looked besides himself with rage. "It's not her fault", Levian managed to mutter as he woke up only to fall back unconscious. "SO LEVIAN KNEW?", Grayson was horrified. Everyone was. Zara and Olive kept their distance from me avoiding eye contact. "This has been a wonderful birthday thanks guys, it's better we never see each other again. I mean come on a water monster, a couple that has too many issues, a drunkard and smokers? All this isn't good for my health", Patrick groaned. "Nooo. I'm sorry I didn't mean for this to happen. I forgot I wasn't allowed near water… I don't know what's happening. Nooo". The vision blurred out for me as I stared at Levian's limp body crying as golden mist evaporated from my body.

CHAPTER 10

In Sickness and in Feigned Love

"Okay that's all Esme, let's get you out", Levian said kindly as he helped me out of the Rotating Liah. "The memory is over, you can rest". I rested my head on my palms. "I'm so sorry, that was dreadful, we lost all our friends thanks to me that day".

"Esme, darling that wasn't your fault. It was inevitable and I know this time the memory reset serum is perfected that Abilo gave you but we didn't lose our friends, they came around later", he said stroking my hair. "Levian, I didn't mean to hurt you", I said dejectedly and he put his arms around me smelling like daisies and construction if there were ever an odder mix. I felt safe in his embrace and cried softly watching my tears fall on his shirt.

Levian wiped the tears from my face and kissed my forehead. "You've never hurt me; I was a foolish teenage boy who thought drinking was going to help me deal with losing my parents ever since they were murdered. You helped me through a lot even if you don't remember".

"I wish I could remember more but Aunt Brie never told me about losing me one time. No wonder she was horrified when I went to the lake. I thought after I destroyed Kipsy

City, I was directly living with her in Abilo. ", I said. My whole life was so confounding.

"Well, I know you had another incident in your aunt's city which is why they shut it off to people and perfected their memory serums. You left Kipsy for good then".

That did make sense. The people of Abilo always seemed to fear me and it wasn't just because of the Kipsy incident. I had to get my facts sorted and I needed The Rotating Liah for that. "Levian, I need to see more of my memories", I begged. "The more clues I can get, I can fix the damage I have caused. Please just take me through every moment". Levian smiled a little wistfully. "Yes, I shall, they may get worse but I hope you get closure". "But first, you must rest, todays been a lot for you". He was firm so I relented.

Levian showed me to a little spare bedroom adjacent to the Rotating Liah construction, it was demure in its complexion but radiated plenty of personality with its sky-blue walls and light-yellow shade. "There was one thing I was curious about though", I said frowning. "HB? Who was he and why did all our friends hate him?". Levian raised his eyebrows at me. "You know with all the things you've been through; this was one very interesting time for you. He passed me a granola bar which I nibbled on confused. "Gobble it up, if you want to see what happened with HB, you'll need your energy to go back in there". I nodded and swallowed the bar whole as Levian guided me to the rotating light.

"You ready? I won't be with you in as much of this memory, but I'll be there don't worry". He reassured me. I was ready. I stepped into the Liah once more and shut my eyes as the world around me spun once again, the granola bar suddenly feeling very heavy in the pit of my stomach.

I opened my eyes and saw myself once again. The familiar dark hair, blue eyes. A sudden bolt of energy I had never been accustomed to. That was me at 15, I was suddenly, profoundly industrious and emulsifying this ball of light that travelled everywhere with me. The disdained figure of HB loomed before me, and even as an onlooker from an old memory, I felt like a twinge of annoyance looking at him. The Liah must have erased any memories of the relationship I shared with him because all I could perceive from this direction was the aftermath of the situation.

HB walked up to me just then saying, "Esme, I always knew you were still in love with him but he doesn't deserve you, not after he broke your heart. I had to watch out for you, I had to hack into your dorm's cameras just to keep you safe. Your freedom is my priority, but you couldn't take care of yourself as well as my skills could. I had to protect you from him and I hope you realised that". A bubbling burst of confusion and fury filled me up. It must have rained just then because my dark hair was wet and my skin felt damp and mucky. A powerful twitch in my fingers alerted my thoughts. Water contacts again, I realised. That's all I needed.

"You didn't have to use whatever freakish skill you had to try to control me HB", I said in steady politeness, a psychopathic glint blinging in my eye. I was controlling the twitching in my fingers; I couldn't hurt HB. "Aaron is the REASON I had to Esme, I'm in love with you and I couldn't have disturbed all that, plus I always knew he wouldn't work out so I set it up so YOU WOULD FALL IN MY ARMS and it's working!", the latter retorted, a conspicuous look of dismay now forming on his face.

I was distracted. Aaron, was the only boy I believed I had ever been close to loving. Felt like a dream after all this while yet it dawned in front of me like a candle well-lit and reminiscent of its familiar scent despite its continuous flicker. It was months ago but Aaron was that one phase in my life I would never truly forget. All these years, I held myself in the greatest strength to protect myself and the people from me. What happened to Kipsy City? I was aware and I knew my Aunt Brie meant well but the memory-altering serum hadn't worked on me because I remembered everything. I may have been stunned by the horrors of every waking breath but that didn't mean I couldn't face it each day I woke up.

Boarding school isn't the best solution. Certainly not one albeit the toughness of your situation, whether that involves a faulty memory serum or an accidental tendency for serial killing through inexplicable water powers from a cruel federation feared by the same city. Did I remember what happened before Aunt Brie? Vaguely, I did remember the Hallows. I would dream about it each night, the night I wiped out the entire city and all those days I would get beaten to a pulp and starved till I nearly saw the whites in my eyes from weakness. I would always fight for my life and now the pain just replayed in my memory and no serum would amend that. I was nearly sixteen and although I dreaded my birthday because Gregnich and Madame Hallow would always increase the tolerance of their physical torment, ever since boarding school and Aunt Brie's intervention, I was saved from any further attacks.

Trouble was, I didn't know what to do and my whole unscrambled life, distorted as it was while I tried to piece my memory together, would make a bit more sense if I still talked to my best friend Levian or anyone else in our little friend circle. Of course, Aaron was quite the matter for he had been my first kiss. I loved how his hands felt on my waist, the bliss I entered when he held my hand tightly, almost protecting me from the world, and the sparks that nearly caused fires between the bridges of our mouths as our eyes locked on to each other's as two poles, opposite yet drawn to each other with steady affluence. He tasted like a poison mixed with its nectar. It was both stifling yet so purely fervent in a procedure that it kept me wrapped around the heat of his body, however, incensed its end got me, it had been one of the most adventurous times of my life.

"Earth to Esme", HB annoyingly said, calling me back to the present state. I laughed causing a vivid look of confusion on his face. "You tried to possess me, own me even". I said to the rather astute boy. "You watched my every waking move, you hacked into cameras which went against all laws of my privacy and you used blackmail to your technical advantage against my friends and me. All this because you were insecure that I wasn't over Aaron? I sounded more incredulous that I felt. The Head Boy may have been my largest relationship error because he transpired to be the most unsettling version of a stalker any teenager would care to have. "It's not just Aaron or those friends of yours", he declared. "It's almost every other guy who becomes an admirer for you in mere moments and while I agree it's because of sparkplug spirit, mind, personality and invigorating beauty. It is frustrating to know that I can never have you all to myself". I hadn't known what to say and while the constant stream of admirers he so freely spoke about was *more* than an over-exaggeration when the boys who actually noticed me were at nothing, he wasn't wrong about Aaron, my heart had only belonged to him as I watched him stamp on it a few months ago which eventually led me to date HB and indulge in a senseless teenage rebound who lacked the essential entertainment and made me wish I had never met him in my life.

"I'm sorry HB but we're broken up and you have to admit to yourself that we'll never be together again. Give my regards to Aaron when you do see him", I said politely and he slammed his wallet into the ground, a feat that was intriguing to watch. "Yes, because you'll just go crawling back to him, won't you?", said he and proceeded to grab me by the shoulders which I deflected. "Aaron and I are over. He never truly exists in my life but whatever toxicity lies between us, it fails to affect me". Those might have been my last proper words to HB and I meant them. Aaron was that guy whose conversation I couldn't even remember after the serum's second effect yet I remembered him somehow and his meddling in my life as a constant stream after he alluded me with the truth of me just being a one-time event in his life and we were well and truly over.

I clutched my stomach suddenly and threw up all over the floor and caught my reflection in the bathroom mirror where I went to wash my face and mainly get away from

HB. Memories of Aaron holding me and piling food onto my plate as I clumsily tried to swallow each morsel caught up with me and I gagged, a puddle of salivary morsels with the most pervasive stench erupted from me and I stared onward at my reflection, tears of pain streaming from my eyes, burning with each drop. My body was mere ribs, my face mere cheekbones and the jet-black hair was weak and stringy as large clumps of it fell out more than I could count. My eyes were heavy and pained from insomnia, the dreams kept me alive each night, monstrosity of them got so real that sleep had become a distant relative I had lost that year. I wetted my hands slightly with the water and drew them at the mirror, the golden magic beaming and uncovering my true reflection. This time I saw differently. It wasn't the pale, frail little girl standing in front of me, sleep deprived and weary of exhaustion and anorexia. It was the face of the most roguish monster I had seen. The ears stretched into large, dagger -shaped instruments, the head was a crown for all satanic devils and the mouth... My word, the mouth and cheeks were carved into a pointed hiss while my eyes shone with red, hot blood reflecting on all the people in Kipsy City I had killed those years ago with my magic.

I transformed the reflection back to my face and hastily stuffed the whole ham sandwich I had packed for my lunch only to momentarily vomit it out in the toilet. I clutched my stomach, silently screaming in agony. My brain was dizzy and feeble and suddenly, I felt no energy to get up and move. I grabbed my bag and attempted to walk out of the bathroom but I slipped. The last thought that crossed my mind was the picture of Aaron putting even proportions of food onto my plate. He had taken care of me as a gym freak who took great care of his intake, He had greatly helped me in getting healthier but now I had fallen back to my old ways and it wasn't entirely because of him. The nightmares at night had removed my need for food. In the brightest way possible, the fainting from anorexia would at least get me some more sleep.

The memory suddenly altered its directions and seemed to be travelling in a flash forward to three months later. I shut my eyes tightly and clutched at my already growling stomach. This memory seemed different. It was in a classroom with the most peaceful woman I had ever seen in my life, all my other friends stood around her. The girls had tears in their eyes and the boys stood grim-faced. I didn't quite know what to feel. Letting the memory sink in was quite time-consuming in the Liah.

CHAPTER 11

Asylum Therapy

Post-traumatic stress makes things different. It conveys a youth of pain, pressure and every metaphorical needle that could prick you at the slightest. There I was. Standing in front of my beloved teacher on her last day of school as she uttered her final words to all of us. No, this wasn't in the Liah. It was just a memory hitting me like the vivid flashback of the van hitting Grayson as he fell unconscious at my feet as I tried to escape the yellow, Chinese monster on the chain bound tightly to my throat.

This was a different memory. I was in a white-washed office facing a medical professional. The office looked more like a cage than an office until it hit me. It wasn't an office; it was an asylum. I was finally once again perceived as a threat to humanity and all its black- and-white pieces. Sixteen years old and yet it wasn't a needle that pricked me to my eternal slumber. It wasn't a romantic thriller straight out of sixteen candles or the Sound of Music. It was life. My life to be exact and it wasn't the movie I ever saw it to be.

"You're in safe hands Esme, you can let go", the professional said gently piercing me with her judging grey eyes that gave me pity and fear at the same time. I heard myself laugh coldly. I sounded different, there was raw emotion in my voice, and

I barely recognized it. I wasn't frightened by the powers that consumed me with half a memory. It had seized control of its chaos, control of its darkness and wore it like a shattered clock ticking to keep alive. For the first time since I was in the Liah, it wasn't just a memory the Liah was repeating for me. This was an amalgam of a flashback and a well-produced memory. Or maybe it was the same logic of water storing memory? Because here in the asylum, I recalled everything before the first memory serum and now I could sort out pieces of my memory before the stronger memory serum.

I was the monster I saw in the mirror; I had accepted it. Long fishnet gloves adorned my palms, darkened and calloused from the water magic. I must have used it a few times with perfect control. It wasn't the old version of me in the memory. It was really me. I was just the same age as she. "There's nothing I can do to let go", I uttered stoically. "If I was good at school before, my brain's not up to cope with it now because of all the memory testing and torture I have had to endure". "And you're keeping my aunt away from me too and pretending she's dead when I know she isn't no matter what you show me. I have magic in me, I'm not going to fall for it". My voice was deep and controlled but the hysteria scattered across it was reckless.

"What was the memory of your Miss Thea? You seem to have shared a special bond with her right?", the professional asked. I looked away. Yes, Miss Thea had been close to me. She shared a special bond with my friends and me until the Hallows decided to finish off with her. "It was her last day", I began. "She was leaving school and she was saying goodbye to all of us and she had the wisest words

I could never forget for us all". I closed my eyes to imagine it playing out before me.

There she was, the plump, jolly woman with the sweetest smile and most magnificently arched eyebrows. She gave all of us some beautiful descriptions. My friend group was on the verge of breaking at that point, and it could have been my magic's fault. It was pure chaos but it got resolved somehow. A lot had happened since that talk. I had fallen head over heels for Grayson and the love I gained for him allowed me to feel more at peace in my head. Miss Thea might have increased it in her description for him when she turned to him and gave him her last words. Grayson's was beautiful, almost too beautiful to mention and the truth in it was handsome beyond compare. I could feel myself falling in love then and I was okay with it.

Levian's was hilarious and a magnificent way to joke around with such vigorous emotion being played around. Marshall's followed with a pinch of salt, as beautiful as Grayson's and Patrick's? The accuracy of her words to him was not just advice. It was eye-opening! Olive and Zara followed in definite pride but mine. I adored it. I did remember what she said to everyone but a little part of me wished to keep that to myself only and never mention it ever again. My description however was noteworthy of mentioning. "Esmerliah", Miss Thea pronounced my name like royalty. "You're worth so much more than words. You keep me alive with your curiousness yet profound wisdom". All my friends were now staring at me, everyone was taken aback by emotion and I had never felt closer to them than I did just then. "I was afraid to teach you, one of River Valley's stars, your ingenuity is difficult to teach but you gave me happiness to teach you. The fusion of childlikeness and wisdom is so intense that it makes the whole world open up to you and love you. No more so, the ones that bring chaos in you because you wouldn't let anyone cause you chaos in the world but your own mind and when it does descend into chaos, remember it's because you're letting go onto a new path because that's the level of courage and strength you will always have".

Opening my eyes back to the asylum, the chaos had descended in me and the control was away from my head but my body ceased to fight now. It just wanted to remain at peace. "What happened with Grayson?", The professional intervened and I scowled shooting a bolt of yellow light directly above her head realising that she was in a well-protected glass cage so I couldn't hurt her. "It's a memory, I'm showing you a symbol", I snarled disdainfully as I wrapped my gloved fingers around a ball of yellow light and enlarged it, focusing the light to show an image of Grayson and I, our heads together, sitting close and smiling at the camera.

In school, I had fallen in love with Grayson. Trying to control my water magic was difficult but with Grayson, he was my happy place. When he looked into my eyes, I saw heaven lift me from hell. I had known him for a while but now he consumed every bone of mine. He brought me peace and I wasn't constantly swivelled in a world of mayhem. We shared each other's company quite a lot around the time we turned 16,17. He made me see the world through a sense of both comfort and fight and I adored the fight and strength in him because it made me believe in my own, in my control over my magic. He never judged me and made me feel loved and this instant connection we suddenly achieved was too good to be true. Aaron wasn't love for me, Grayson was both physical and spiritual love I had never experienced before. That kind of story doesn't time too well with a life of an apparent monster and it was proved right in time. Patrick's celebrations may have been cursed because he threw a huge party that my friends and I went to along with a few more people we all mutually knew. I went with control in my exterior, dressed up and excited to see Grayson and the rest of my friends and the people we were partying with. What started as the night of my life ended in terror that day. Grayson and Zara started liking each other and I confessed to Olive that I liked Grayson. The second blow after Patrick's birthday occurred when Olive went directly to Grayson and conveyed my secret which blew up in my face because Grayson knew after he and Zara got together humbled my confidence a great deal and in my eyes Olive betrayed me. Marshall as Olive had suspected was secretly in love with Zara too and I was introduced to both my first heartbreak and love square that I wasn't winning.

It wasn't like I wasn't attractive to other people. Albeit being heartbroken and disastrously drunk at the same time, Levian comforted me but he was hanging out with Olive which incensed Marshall a slight bit. Needless to say, the night got a lot worse when a drunk creep started passing me the stare of perversion, walking up behind me and I held Levian's hand the whole night to protect myself to which he kindly obliged. Not the best teenage party. Matters got worse when I allowed every bit of ache in me to completely take control over me and I caused glowing golden roped out of nowhere to settle themselves down on the grown, one pulling Zara's hair out and the other brandishing a golden knife at the perverted creep. The night haunted me for weeks after that especially dealing with Grayson and Zara's new relationship that haunted both Marshall and me. They didn't last very long and ended up breaking up three months after they started dating when Grayson decided to pursue a different girl and Zara was too well focused on her house being taken away from her and her family. I never knew which girl Grayson liked but the heartbreak he caused me unintentionally was delirious to my magic. If it felt like we had moments, I knew it was true.

"When did you start realising you weren't the same in your head?", the professional asked me placidly. This therapy session bored me to bits. "There was a Hallows sighting in Kipsy that brought great terror to the townsfolk. They tracked me down when I was at Levian's house and found the secret tunnel. Gregnitch stabbed a knife into my wrist but at that time, I was apathetic to pain. My threshold was higher than anyone's". "What else happened, you go silent when you're asked to describe the episodes of violence turned to you?".

I sucked the inside of my skin flicking sparks of light every now and then from my fingers. "Gregnitch found Miss Thea and told me I couldn't run away so easily. It was the Hallow's plan to confine the whole city to one giant concentration camp. He tied me up to a metal chair in a cage much like this one with less oxygen so I wasn't strong enough to get up or make any fuss. He stabbed the knife into her throat and pulled it out and did it once more for me to watch". "I could do nothing". I zapped a little lightning bolt from my fingers and flung them across the room watching them collide with each other. Truth was, after my blood spilt everywhere that day, I was weak at my knees and felt myself disintegrating somehow.

Everything after that was a whirl. I got ominous voices in my head laying scenarios that would cause me to zone out and listen to them. They were violent voices. I saw moats on fire, and my friends dying, and I got a thousand headaches because of how loud the voices were. I never knew what a panic attack was, but I felt an internal pain that controlled my every move. It was like having pressure down my throat and it stopped my breathing flow. I couldn't sleep at night and I would wake up each day alarmed after each nightmare although the reality was no dream either. I found myself mixing up my head with reality, and it caused more chaos in me. I isolated myself from the world, not wanting to hurt anyone or see more people get hurt because of me. Miss Thea's disappearance had created a huge mystery in the town as people tried to search for her and I kept the secret, my head held high when internally my body contorted in pain. I was a wreck until I felt tears falling down my cheeks and by using them, I developed even stronger magic. Blasting the school of its hinges was what got me sent to the asylum in the first place. The times the anger and anxiety hit were when I locked myself in the cupboard, my legs banging against in sides, the pain inside me defeating me as light spread all around me, glowing in emotion but it was way too strong. It spread across the school like poison and blasted it. It was thankful that it was empty that day so nobody got hurt.

"Well when someone like you has post-traumatic stress disorder, you're not going to be let loose are you? You should try writing about it so you could process your feelings and even remember incidents connected with it.", the professional said getting up. She was wrong. I needed to be free after feeling trapped from every end. I needed to be freed from the voices in my head. I was in pain beyond my capacity and nobody understood it. Writing seemed like a poor substitute, a random advocate for change with zero effect. For the first time in my life, being alone felt like horror to me. I needed someone to calm me down and cure me. I was always alone but now that Aunt Brie wasn't there either, I was really all by myself and I felt sick to my stomach. I gagged on air, breathed dust and felt no presence of any sort. I was finally insane and suffering.

CHAPTER 12

Back at Brie's

The asylum was pure horror. I must have been there for around two weeks and my head was swallowing itself in half already. Every dream was a reoccurring nightmare for the two solemn hours of sleep I would get each day. Treated like a monster and yet all I craved for was affection. They showed me evidence of Aunt Brie's body at the time. I was never told about how she died but it was a situation of great alarm and the voices in my head disallowed me from processing reality too much.

By far the worst thing that could have happened to me while I was trapped. The voices in my head brought the clearest pictures of things I didn't wish to think about. Love being one of them. I had been a victim and a cause of violence for as long as I remembered. It was unusual that my brain could also be succumbed to love. While in the asylum, my brain travelled to the most extraordinary facets it had ever approached. I remembered Levian just then. I felt safe with him. He gave me shelter away from the Hallows. He held my hand when I felt scared or disconsolate, I was at peace and I felt slightly less alone. He was my best friend in the whole world and there would never be a soul who knew me better than he did and I missed him dreadfully. Even the love I had for Grayson could not account for that. Nothing ever could although it left me heartsick. They released me in three days when I passed the asylum's safety protocols. What kept me from blowing off sparks was thinking about Levian. It calmed me down and I missed him terribly. After being estranged and left to survive all by myself, he was the comfort I needed that he had given me, and I yearned for that with the strictest passion. I was right about Aunt Brie as well. As soon as I was released from the asylum, a few officials came up to me with my beloved Aunt Brie, wanting to take me in again far away from Kipsy City. What I didn't immediately recognise back then was that they were actually from the adoption agency. Aunt Brie took me back home but this time what should have felt like extraordinary gaiety and comfort felt eldritch. It felt like the person who had lived with her before was a different person and not me.

Aunt Brie had legally adopted me through the agency and they promised to take good care of me and my powers as long as I was dosed with their new memory serum. I would be saying goodbye to everything that belonged to my old life of course but considering I hadn't been dosed yet, I was in a completely different state of mind.

"You'll be okay Esme darling, I'm just thrilled you're with me again!", Aunt Brie said enveloping me with a warm side hug. I remembered her scent well. It was of old books and the daisies she would collect every morning. I remembered sliding into a paroxysm of congeniality by it but right now, sixteen-year-old me only felt like the person who did live with her was different. I felt like an imposter. On the drive home, I remembered each bend. The blue and white borders of the roundabout islands that led to Abilo and the steady stream of sunlight that lit up my room at Aunt Brie's house from the large balcony door. It embarrassed me to think I was actually apprehensive. My hand grazed the bookshelf where Aunt Brie added all my favourite books after she rescued me from the Hallows back when I was a mere slip of a girl. The fondness of the memory welled tears in my eyes, its golden rims sparkling with a faint flicker of golden light. Yet there was one problem. I didn't feel the memory, I only remembered it. Whoever I was before. Before all the memory serums, torment, high school drama and monster magic, wasn't me. It was somebody else and I was the falsetto head who was just taking up her place because that girl had died long since.

Aunt Brie's eyes looked more hollowed and she looked much older. That impish grin she always wore had disappeared and was replaced with a stout line that would curve up to a smile from time to time. I almost didn't know what to say to her, she looked like a stranger and my head felt completely disconnected. The voices in my head continued their stiff menagerie, howling at my reality. I felt alone and yearned for Grayson. The same Grayson who dated Zara. Unrequited it may be, but Grayson had been the one for me and I had fallen head over heels for him. The way my eyes felt when they peered into his. The way my stomach churned when he put his head against mine to hug me. Grayson was exactly what I had needed to deal with my magic to pace me down. It was what I required urgency to silence the voices in my head. All I wanted was to feel loved and less alone and with Aunt Brie's unfamiliar yet memory -sparking presence, I was in a whirlwind of confusion and chaos and I was so sick of it.

Living itself was suffering. Whatever control or strength I had dominated into my system perished with the present suffering. Waking up to anguish each day. Falling asleep to nightmares each night. What was the point? I tried to chase the beauty of life and yet always managed to get hauled into the darkness. I just couldn't tolerate the pain anymore. I refused to. And here it went again, another memory serum to forget about the life that never left me behind. What should I wish for? Grayson to forget all about Zara and realise that there was nobody he'd rather be with than my own distorted, magical self? Levian to continue providing me with refuge whenever I needed it EVEN THOUGH I KNEW HE WAS IN LOVE WITH ME. For Aunt Brie to give out cupcakes while I helped them land on my friend's plates with exquisite control using my water blast powers? Maybe in a different reality, all of these things would be possible. Facing the Hallows and locking them up, gave Kipsy City the freedom, it deserved. In a different reality, all these things would be apt.

CHAPTER 13

The Fear of Remembering

Fear is what consumes you. It eats you up until you're so lathered up in trepidation that you build yourself an armour. A guard of some sort. That's what I had done to myself. The years after I was taken away from Aunt Brie, I lost all hope I had. There was not a single bite of happiness left for me to savour. All I could see was the red and green light of pain flashing before my eyes, flickering until I gave up and screamed to release some of it.

I could never let go of it. My guilt for what I had done to Kipsy City. Remembering the fear, I had in each encounter with the Hallows and every time I couldn't control my magic with my friends. Every one of these grief-stricken traumatic incidents bashed the life out of me. "You can't survive without just living Esme", Levian told me the last time we were! together. "You need to live because you're happy". I had lost track of happiness until Aunt Brie rediscovered me again. Walking through the oddly familiar halls of her house again after 3 years was an oddity. I remembered feeling happiness three years ago when I was living with her but not being able to feel that same feeling reminded me of the icy shards of pain that built up in my stomach. In my heart.

Aunt Brie made me a lemon tart. One of my favourites because no faulty memory serum can separate favourite foods from a human when humans recognise the taste and smell of foods, they like using their receptors. She smiled at me, encouraging me to eat it so I did as she continued frying the beetroot cutlets she was frying, another one of my old favourites. My mouth melted in satisfaction. I felt at home again, I felt less of a need to fight and I certainly felt a peaceful bubble soar across my head, replacing the anxious cloud that always popped in every situation. I was slowly embracing my present. I never ever wanted to go back to Kipsy City, to that pure curse of a place despite Levian, despite Grayson or anyone I had ever grown to love there. The Harbour federation may have granted me my powers, believing I could become a weapon overnight, but I surpassed that control by reasoning with that belief. I was just a child and now as a young girl trying to find peace where she could, those powers are rendered useless to me forever and I didn't mind not being able to harness them ever.

I didn't want to see any more pain. The slow moments of happiness I had with Aunt Brie at her house were all I wanted for the rest of my life. I was ready to forget every single god forsaken moment where I was running on constant adrenaline, trying to control the world around me with those blasts of light erupting from my hands and eyes. "I'm ready", I suddenly said dropping my second tart. I looked at Aunt Brie intensely, trying out the deepest fixture my voice could reach. She arched her left eyebrow. "Are you quite certain my love?", she asked me. "What about your friends? You won't remember anything; you'll never be able to use those ever again". I looked at my fingers sparking a hole in the tablecloth.

Control had always been my desire. Ironically, I could not deliver it when it came to my powers. Considering Abilo's perfected memory serum for just me, I was nearly desperate to forget and only remember my life at Abilo no matter what I had to sacrifice. I remembered Grayson and how I felt when my love for him wasn't reciprocated when he led me on but loved Zara instead. How I felt when I hurt Levian, when my whole friend group fell apart that day on Patrick's birthday and how every relationship, I had gotten into were just strings in a babbling ball of chaos.

I could never stop loving Grayson and Levian was much better off without me. I had made up my mind. I wanted to forget it all and move on in this new life of mine as a normal girl who was loved by her Aunt. I was ready to take the serum. Aunt Brie had already sorted out all the paperwork with the Abilo agency and they began the process rapidly, inserting the copper-coloured liquid into serums that they were about to inject into me. Aunt Brie wanted to hold my hand but I was immune to pain. I told her to let go and settled myself for what was to come. They say you can see your whole life flash by as memories when you're about to lose them. That may be the worst lie you've ever told because all I saw was what mattered to me. Aunt Brie, my new life without any pain. I felt my head getting clearer as the serums were injected into my arms and legs. The faint golden sizzle that sparked between my fingers was disappearing and my arm muscles started to pulse. It was happening, I was forgetting about everything. Not a second more and all the pain would be washed away into the serum and I would be living happily ever after. The ceiling became dark all of a sudden and I could not see or hear a thing but the bubbling sound of silence. I had finally passed out.

The silence that beamed around me was claustrophobic, almost deafening and possessive at the same time. A warm feeling crept up my neck and surrounded my body. If I wasn't passed out already, this would have surely done the trick. Nothing made sense all of a sudden. It was like my whole brain was slowly being sizzled and washed out until it was squeaky clean. Not that I was complaining of course. The last thing I could recall hearing was the queer, faint sound of someone gagging and the vibrations in my ear from the silence taking off like a plane at 3 am. Weird analogy yet effective to describe some of the planes that took off in Abilo. I always found them most luring because of how distant they seemed from the rest of the world. Their lack of staying grounded because they were so high up that they would prevail to the heavens above, supercilious but intrepid. I always envied them, wishing I was up there with them but I had never been on a plane before.

Something clicked and I fell to my feet and opened my eyes momentarily. Present day Levian was fanning my head and the vibrations I felt a second ago in my ear could be heard again. "Wha- who- huh?", I spoke slowly. I tried to shake off the sound of silence my ear was filled with not wanting to go uncharacteristically deaf. "You're okay, I've got you", Levian said gently as he helped me up to his comfortable, zebra-patterned armchair. The black and white sent my head spinning even further. "You electrocuted the Liah with your magic, I'll fix it later but it must have hurt your head, are you okay?". His kind eyes were fixed on me, his veritable concern calming me down. "Levian", I whispered. "I remember everything now. The serum was given only to me and it was quite strong so everyone knew what I was except me for the final time. AND IT WAS LAST YEAR". Levian put his arms around me, placing his chin on my head, stroking my head ever so slightly as I sobbed uncontrollably.

He didn't say a word, not that there was anything he could have said that would reduce the complication of the last few years and my entire life but either way my knees felt stronger and my body felt less liquid like now. "So, you really do remember everything now? That water magic must have really undone the serum work", Levian finally spoke, fetching me a glass of water. "They didn't tell us anything about you but the Hallows entered school, made a bit of a fuss and when they couldn't find you, you were pronounced dead to the news, and they took off. The Harbour Federation fell completely but it also left Kipsy in damage so after the first bombing, everyone moved to other places. We had college anyway. "So why are you here? Isn't it the middle of senior year?", I asked puzzled. I hadn't seen a soul when I entered Kipsy City with Betty except for the police officers and the little rat Felis.

"They shifted school to Salt Lake, it's a district in the outskirts that's right next to Kipsy but didn't suffer any of the damage. We're quite close to Detroit. I never moved because after Kipsy was safe enough to inhabit despite its muck, I couldn't leave the Liah or the place, it was my home and the last reminder of my parents". Levian had read my mind. "So, do you want to see everyone again? Make sure they know you aren't dead, Salt Lake isn't too far from here", I really appreciated the suggestion because it had been so long. "Wait Levian, I'd love to but first, I left a friend of mine back in my old house with the caretaker, Felis and my aunt must be worried sick after I left her that note so maybe I could do some damage control first". He smiled and squeezed my hand. I don't know why a jet of electricity passes my hand every time he touches it. I assumed it to be my powers. "I can come with you, I know Felis and the police officers here, I'm sure they'd let your friend be, everyone's still pretty worked up after everything that happened last year and we don't want another Harbour Federation reminder". It hit me all of a sudden. "They think I was one of the bad guys?", I asked incredulously. The Hallows enslaved me to their purpose and I was tortured for years and kidnapped. I had PTSD for crying out loud! I don't know why I was taking my frustration out on Levian. He graciously allowed my reaction until he led my way out of the door. I stopped him.

"Wait I have an idea", I said. From whatever I had learned in the last few days, it was that water had memory and connections which meant I could communicate with Betty without going to her directly. "I spilt some of Levian's water from the glass on the floor and ignoring his gasp of surprise, I closed my eyes and imagined Betty's face in the lake we were in at Abilo. Sure enough, Betty's wizened yet beautiful face stared back at me, she seemed semi-solid which meant she was no longer in trouble. "Hi Betty, just wanted to let you know that I'm safe and I got my memory back but I also need to sort out a few things before I do anything. How's the situation at your end?", I said as her cheeky grin twinkled back at me. There was something about Betty that was irresistible. She said the most absurd things but you couldn't help liking her despite her villain- like antics. “I’m glad to hear ya say that girlie. I took care of Felis, and got out at the first sight of water and these little lads just stared dumbfounded. Who’s the hottie behind ya?”, Her face loomed larger as I kept the communicator open with my hands as they glowed a bright golden.

I looked at Levian behind who was staring like he saw a ghost. I couldn’t blame him; Betty did say she was a fugitive from the Harbour Federation and she probably scared a lot of people in her day anyway. “Betty, I need you to do something for me, I left my aunt a note back at Abilio in the lake I first saw your face in and I need you to make sure she’s okay and doesn’t come back here. You can take Ambrosia with you”, I said as the horse who had been asleep for the longest time woke up with a start after hearing her name. “You’re trusting a murderer from the mythical dark side”, Levian muttered disdainfully. He seemed to have regained the ability to speak. Betty gave me another one of her cheeky grins. “Hey no fair boy, Esmerliah over here has her fair share of the dark side, there’s no judging me but why are ya trusting me girlie, I’m a stranger you met from the dark side as this smart young un says”

It was a good question. Betty Harbour should be the last person I trust but she had been kind to me and allowed me to figure out who I was when I was left confused and haunted by my powers. In a way, she had helped me much better than anybody else I knew and I couldn’t help liking her. It was never her fault that she had been forced to live her life like this. She was young and she did what she had to do until the Hallows set out to kill her as well. I couldn’t pity her because Betty Harbour was the last person anyone could lend pity to but my gut told me she could be trusted. Maybe it was that sharp twinkle in her eye. "Betty, we're the same kind as you said, we've both been used by the Federation and hunted down by the Hallows. I trust you to do this for me and we can both find our way back". She nodded and with one large swoop, the water, now taking the shape of her slender body wrapped itself around the confused Ambrosia pulling her into the small puddle before disappearing completely. Just like that, the two of them were gone, I sighed, I hoped Betty could be trusted and my gut wasn't being hypnotised by whatever else Betty's powers could do.

"So, I see you replaced me with a fugitive as a best friend but I see you have control over the monster magic now", Levian teased. "Oh well, takes one supernatural being to know another", I quipped as we set out to go to Salt Lake. I couldn't help but worry about Aunt Brie but Levian's reassuring arm that slid around my waist as we stepped outside his home calmed me down and sent a tingly sensation down my back. He spun me around hesitantly and placed his hands on my sides and traced one hand slowly up, cupping my face. "Hey, Esme I can't tell you happy I am to have you here with me right now, I don't want to ever lose you again". My face burned a bright red just then as I looked back into his eyes which were fixated on my own. "Me too", I said, my voice unusually high. "So, what memory do you see when you're alone in the Liah?", I asked changing the subject, a defence mechanism that I now remembered using quite often. Levian frowned. He knew what I was doing. Of course, he did. "It's just one memory, I don't have the water magic to show me multiple Esme".

I placed my hand on him, his palm hadn't left my cheek yet. "Hey, Betty's quite pretty isn't she, want a date with the beautiful, magical creature?", I asked quite obnoxiously. My brain wished for me to get out of the intimate region it had stumbled across and the warm feeling of butterflies acting like their behinds were on fire in my stomach persisted. "She really is but not more so than you", he said in his deep voice as he let go of me and we walked out his back door, ready to get into a compact, red car all the way to Salt Lake. I got in with him and gave his hand a squeeze, a bright smile playing on my face and I hoped he couldn't hear the delirium of butterflies in my stomach. They were so loud; it was possible the whole city could hear them. My smile faded when I glanced at Levian and realised he must have missed me quite a bit. It also struck the same agony that I had left him and everyone and allowed myself to forget all of them, especially Levian willingly just to go back to Abilo and live in peace. A part of me could tell he was hurt but I knew I did care about him and I would have to explain the dilemma behind that confounding choice. Maybe when I saw all our friends again in Salt Lake. I sighed resting my head against the car window. This was going to be an interesting day…

Part 2

The Present

CHAPTER 14

Salt Lake

Salt Lake may not be too far away from Kipsy City but it was still over an hour's drive. Levian had inserted a CD into his car's music player that rang out my favourite song by the Avett Brothers. Heart full of doubt. It had always been my favourite song, even the memory serum hadn't been enough to wipe the country, the electric guitar's strumming out of my head. Levian smiled at me as I stared outside the passenger window, murmuring the lyrics. '*There's a darkness in me that's flooded in light*'. I couldn't agree with that line more, the light from my powers was just a cover-up for what was real. I could feel his stare burning the back of my head. I returned his smile and continued looking back outside the window. There was nothing but the ruins of Kipsy City that could be seen but it saved me the trouble of starting a conversation with my long-lost best friend or something more as it would seem.

My company seemed to get the hint because he cranked up the music a little louder and the drive continued in silence. Time always sponsors introspection. Right now, I wasn't thinking about my friends, or Kipsy City or the Harbour Federation and the Hallows. I was only thinking about my Aunt Brie and Abilo. She must have been through so much just taking me under her care, adopting me despite me being precarious for her and her amicable little city. I loved everything about Abilo, and in a strange way, I kind of missed it. I adored our little cottage. The yellow walls, and the white tiled ceiling that I would often wonder what it looked like if the whole cottage was flipped upside down and if we had the tiles for flooring instead.

The stoned structured flooring that I would walk on every day barefoot, lounging around in my alluring, chiffon, flowy dresses that Aunt Brie always so carefully picked out for me according to my own choice. The sturdy dining table we'd sit on and sip our tea every evening, eating lemon tarts and cakes as Aunt Brie would tell me magnificent stories about my name and the enchantments about my mother. I knew the Hallows weren't my real parents but I was pretty sure I was created at the federation as a designer baby when all the experiments were done on me. I shuddered at the memory of the Hallow's house I had passed.

I thought back to when I was eleven when Aunt Brie had first brought me back home. She hadn't a lot of money back then and I had learnt the art of saving up. The Abilo bookstore had been my favourite place to visit. I would be transformed into a new world every single day as I digested every section there faster than most girls my age would buy tasteful designer boots from their favourite stores. I remembered Olive and Zara to be those girls, although Zara had more taste anyway and Olive despite all her wealth, purchased the most garish of things that couldn't be sported as anything else but lurid.

Aunt Brie would lend me pocket money once every week and I would buy as many books as I could. If it were possible to live off books and books alone, I would do it. Most often, I would be done reading the book in the store by the time I purchased it but after I had, I couldn't bear not having the book in my possession. Clothes came by once in two months. Aunt Brie took up sewing at times when I desperately needed new clothes and I would get constant trinkets and jewellery from her own collection that she used to wear when she was younger. She would never treat me as if I were just a child. I was always regarded as an equal and she would pretend I always understood things she discussed, however mature or meticulous the subject was. It's how I learnt to take care of myself at any rate.

I know at present moment, Levian regarded me as taciturn. I was different. Sadness seeps into a person's eyes after they face their brains fighting themselves. Seeing Miss Thea tortured to death in front of my eyes by Gregnitch had taken a lot out of me. Losing Aunt Brie had taken a huge toll on my health, the ability for me to function. My powers hurting people, and being treated like a monster even by my own friends when I lost control increased every health problem that attacked me in the last three years. Memory serums really mess the brain up, even the ones of a water-powered child. It was only natural for me to be less affable. More brooding and silent as I struggled to process reality now, ignoring the constant headaches that would hit me.

I chuckled to myself as the memory, of Aunt Brie laying out lady fingers and garlic on a plate on top of the most beautifully adorned mat, hit me as I bit into 4 chillies at the same time. I loved spicy food. We had been talking about our finances and the mat that had a picture of a teapot and cookies made me imagine a billion stories the mat had been adapted from and for some odd reason, Brie and I could not stop laughing ourselves silly. We planned to save up then for a while and except for walks, I intended on staying home and helping out as much as I could. With less use of gas and electricity when we didn't need it etc. Tears welled up in my eyes for the second time today at the memory. I really hoped she was alright, and Betty had managed things.

"I see misery enjoys silent company", I heard Levian finally say. My eyes did a double take as I was passed back to reality and noticed that we were at a stop light for the last five minutes. "I'm not miserable, I'm just thinking about my aunt, that's all", I reply quickly with a shrug. "Esme, she'll be okay I promise. I would love to meet her when you've settled things down a bit more. She seems to have provided quite well for you; you look happier".

He wasn't wrong, I was much happier at Abilo. I had never been quite as happy at Kipsy ever so I nodded in his direction. There wasn't much conversation after and the only time we spoke next was we arrived at Salt Lake. I could tell it was the outskirts because this place looked indefinitely breath-taking. Birds chirped in tune and I could have sworn I saw a yellow chaffinch hop onto a telegraph line.

Levian pulled up into the driveway of a suburban house and opened my car door as I got out half-dazed. "Where are we?", I asked. "This is Patrick's place. His parents went on a cruise for a while so he has his house all to himself", he responded. "Everyone's here?", I asked still confused. It seemed bizarre that all my friends would be at the same place on the day we went looking for them. Levian took a rectangular device out of his pocket just then and typed in something before shutting it. "Cell phone Esme, I would think most of the world uses one now except for some places and I'm assuming Abilo doesn't. Not that you need one with your water portals and all", he explained. "I was texting Patrick to let us in, they're so gonna be shocked to see you again. We had a mourning session and everything for you since the funeral was too out of the question".

I didn't see why Levian couldn't just ring the doorbell but I didn't say anything. Of course, the Hallows had infiltrated my school with fear at even the mention of me. A tall, muscular boy opened his door for us. He had a broad smile that froze as soon as he saw me. I recognised Patrick all right. From both the Rotating Liah's memory and my own. He was quite handsome still yet his cheeks seemed to have sunk like he had a firm grimace set in place. Patrick had seen quite a bit in the last few years and that was certain. "Esmerliah Hallow?", he asked not quite getting the words out as if my name would automatically summon more demons out of me. Levian on the other hand was almost doubled up with laughter as he pointed to his cell phone which clicked at Patrick's disconcerted face.

"Jesus, this is some great stuff", he said as he pushed aside Patrick and dragged me into the living room with him. Patrick's parents must be rich because his entire house was coated with opulence. Everything matched, and everything looked as if it were made for royalty from the glass everywhere to the marble-coated ceiling. Patrick's stupefied look was replicated by a few more of my friends including Olive, Marshall and Zara who looked at me as if they saw a ghost. Well considering they thought I was dead; I couldn't be too surprised. Grayson had come out from Patrick's kitchen holding out a glass bowl of water. He hadn't seen me yet and spoke to the others. "Guys, I think we should try this outside. This would have been so much more fun with Esme here, she would have made something nice and creepy come out of the water, the devil that she was". I grinned to myself and Levian bit his lower lip trying not to laugh out loud. "What? Why do y'all look like someone died. Okay okay, it's been a year, we can talk about her and not act like it's the end of the world again suddenly". Grayson still hadn't obviously seen me or his steady flow of chatter wouldn't have continued. Zara went pale and began crying,

"Zara, you're still blaming yourself for what happened to her aren't you? Look, Esme never held it against you for dating me and I'm pretty sure she got over me once Levian professed his love for her and all those other things she was doing despite her being completely evil and yeah sure I also held on to my liking for her after we broke up when she died mainly because of that but none of that could have been helped or changed by you", he said firmly and Zara glared at him. Levian had stopped laughing and looked down in shame. "Okay why are y'all so mortified—ohhh" Grayson made a peculiar sound as he finally caught sight of me as I walked up to him. He staggered backwards, the glass bowl falling and shattering to a million pieces as water spilt everywhere, drenching me and making him skid backwards.

Almost as a reflex, I brought my hands up and magicked the water to move, the indestructible golden glow from my hand creating a golden bowl, identical to the one Grayson just destroyed as I moved all the water to the bowl and with another flick of my fingers, moved the shattered piece of glass into a grey wastepaper basket nearby. "There you go", I said in a normal voice as I placed the golden bowl down on the coffee table as if all this were completely normal. I was suddenly aware of everyone staring at me again.

Patrick had walked into the room just in time to see this and he sat himself down on the floor, unable to bear his sturdy weight any longer. "Hi, guys! How are all of you, it's been forever", I said chirpily. "And Grayson, we both know you're the evil one out of the two of us, with all the Hitler and violent talk you do make". I smiled; it was good to be back with my friends again despite their dumbfounded faces. "Oh, and I'm not dead by the way", I added to which Marshall snorted. It took a minute before everyone clamoured on top of me hugging me and bombarding me with questions.

"How are you alive??"

"You can do the whole water magic thing without hurting people now?"

"Are you and Levian finally together?"

"How did you come back? What happened?"

I expected them to have questions but was a bit overwhelmed all the same as they all surrounded me, Olive and Zara crying their eyes out now. “You have the most beautiful blue eyes and they glow golden when the light comes out of you”, Olive said whimsically. “I promise I’ll answer them the best as I can but I need Levian’s help”, I said and Levian nodded as he plopped down next to me and began telling everyone everything prompted by me leaving out some of the parts personal to me and I couldn’t help beaming the whole time. I really had missed my friends. They all looked more sombre now and less wild and I felt sorry that it was my fault for having done this to them. Zara held my arm the entire time and suddenly whispered to me. “Esme, I’ve missed you so much this whole year, I couldn’t live with myself knowing you were gone after I took Grayson away from you and I have been guilty the whole time and I love you so much”, Her voice cracked, she was still crying. I looked at her turned-up nose and innocent brown eyes and put my arm around her. “I love you too Zara”, I whispered. “I forgive you; I never held it against you and we’ll catch up soon don’t worry”. She seemed grateful and I turned my attention back to Levian. I would be lying if I said I missed Zara or any of them when I was under the effect of the memory serum. Life sure had gotten complicated but here I was with the six people I had the most love and amusement with yet the most heart-breaking times as well… Was all really forgotten or was I just starting to remember?

CHAPTER 15

Explosions

"You think I'm really that evil huh?", I teased Grayson after Levian was finished filling our friends in about the reason behind my unanticipated appearance. The latter's cheeks flared a beetroot red. He turned towards me. "Look, Esme, I never meant that. It was always your indomitable will that made you who you are. You never gave up despite what you went through each day". The gravel in his voice had always astounded me, attracted me even but it had been more than a year and I was a different person now. He turned my chin around with his hand, urging me to look into his eyes. "Look at me. The Hallows were awful people and their departure to goodness knows where is what stopped the control, you're safe now and so are we so there's no reason to go on hating them forever".

Marshall cocked an eyebrow at Grayson. "Dude, those people wiped out an entire population, we're lucky to even be alive and nonetheless be going to college next year".

"Marshall, I'm just saying. They're gone for good and we've got our Esme back plus I'm sure they were just dealing with business however wronged they were", Grayson replied.

I don't know if it was the thought of my former caretakers that repulsed me but hearing Grayson utter those words made a part of my heart crack, much more than it had done when he had chosen Zara over me.

"Gregnitch Hallow killed Miss Thea, Grayson", I said quietly, twiddling with the hem of my jersey. "I was forced to watch it, she never disappeared because she was murdered. Levian intertwined his fingers with mine in consolation but I pulled my hand back. I didn't want anyone's comfort at this point. The serum had worked quite effectively when it pushed away memories. Even as I remembered everything now, I could not feel any old forebodings or incandescence. It felt like a distant memory, one that I didn't want to recall.

"So, what next?", Olive asked me. She was the only one who treated me with caution now. My old best friend, now a complete stranger. I could tell, judging from her eyes that she was trying to figure me out. What had changed? What hadn't? If she asked me any questions, I'd supply her with any answers but I couldn't guarantee overfriendliness. A curt tone was all I could muster towards her and it wasn't because it was strange seeing her after so much but it was simply because our friendship sort of just fell apart after Patrick's party when she and Levian hung out, leaving me to have my monstrous blast. I think it flustered me that Levian and Patrick were both here to comfort me whereas my best friend was entirely too busy keeping herself entertained. I didn't blame her; she was getting over Marshall and I never held any angst against her either. We just stopped having things to say to each other and with her being a huge supporter of Zara and Grayson, I didn't feel the need to deal with more heartbreak. Perhaps that's the deal with most friendships, however impenetrable they may appear. You just move on to different times in your life where the need for each other weakens until it becomes disused. Besides I was always closer to Levian.

I knew my friends had suffered great losses too. Much more so than I did although we could all put our heads together for losing Miss Thea. That loss had never been administered, especially since the relationship we had with her was incomparable. Heartache, grief, health issues and struggling seemed to be our core values but we could move past them and I had faith that I could as well. "I want to go to college next year like you guys", I finally said. "Move on with my life and maybe stop bad people in the world now that I can control my magic". I smiled at the end of that statement.

Zara hugged me tightly. "Yes! Oh my god, Esme, you should apply to NYU too!". Typical Zara, she remained bubbly despite everything. "I'm sure we can find you some termite infestation problems to solve", Patrick added giving my hand a squeeze. "Oh god Patrick, what did you really do at the HB's house?", Marshall asked with a groan and everyone laughed. This felt right, it had been terribly long until I felt a sense of purpose. I decided to major in Marine Biology. It would be the most fitting to my situation and maybe I'd learn a trick or two that helped my magic.

I would go to school with everyone else after the weekend after I learnt about the changes and registration but first, I would enjoy this party at Patrick's house hoping nothing goes horribly wrong. The third time could be the charm and there was no way I could lose control over my magic again so it seemed safe enough. I spent the day chatting and reminiscing over old memories and new ones with my friends and we exchanged news about our lives. Marshall had a football scholarship he was aiming for, and Olive had enrolled in a design class. I noticed Zara and Marshall playfully flirting with each other and glanced at Olive. Levian and Patrick were playing a serious game of cards on the floor as everyone sat on Patrick's sofa laughing at every single joke. Even the unfunny ones I stood up to get a drink and Grayson saw me staring at them.

"No, they're not a thing but she does lead him on", he said casually matching my glance as he joined me, pouring me a glass too. "And that doesn't bother you?", I inquired. He shook his head, relaxing his jaw. I had forgotten the sharp cut his chin made with the bottom of his ear. I blinked, hoping Grayson hadn't caught me being enraptured by him completely. He grinned at me as he knew of the thoughts racing in my head. "I'm sorry I didn't give you more thought when I chose Zara, we always did match so perfectly together", he said holding my arm. My arms were folded across my stomach. I shook my head dismissively pardoning him for his gratuitous apology.

"Grayson, I don't blame you. I wasn't ever even mad at you because you couldn't help who you chose to fall for. Besides, we've been friends for seven years and I can't hold it against you. I became okay with you never liking me back.", I uttered swallowing quickly, eager to spurn any grim memories. He watched me keenly and after being satisfied with my candour, he drained his glass and refilled it. "Good. I'm glad we got it past us". He slid his arm around my waist as he walked away and I became intensely aware of his careless arm accidentally hovering lower than my waist. Confusion drowned me which increased after I made the error of calling after him.

"Grayson, do you want another drink?", I asked nervously. I realised this was the same question I kept asking him at Patrick's party last year when I had alcohol burning in my throat, trying my best to flirt with him. The embarrassment crawled into my face again but this time I had a different plan. Grayson got back and took the cup from my hands, not taking his eyes off mine. I poured some water into the cup and dug my hand into it, feeling the tingle in my fingers. I brought them up and made a locket with a gold heart, it had the words 'Z heart G' emblazoned on its middle. "I forgot to give this to you and Zara, I bought one that looked exactly like it for one of your birthdays". Grayson frowned. "I don't want that anymore but you can change it right?".

I nodded and erased the 'Z' from the locket. "Who's the current girl?", I asked a little too inquisitively. "Nobody in particular but you could put the letter E", he responded. My heart skipped a beat. "Eleanor, she's this cute girl in my psychology class", he continued. Of course, why didn't I think of that, I worked towards adding the letter 'E' carefully to the locket. "There you go, that's for you", I said, my voice sounding unnecessarily high-pitched. I detested the effect Grayson always had on me. I was about to walk back when he pulled my arm, pulling me closer to him. "You're still the same Esme, even if you have these fancy new powers you can control and this whole different life. I'm assuming there aren't any Gs in Abilo". His voice muffled against my neck and I could hear his heart beating steadily. Its tone wasn't as sonorous as mine felt and not quite as unsteady or liquid-like.

"How do you know I live in Abilo? Levian didn't mention that", I ask instead furrowing my eyebrows. "Esme, I kept up with you, I didn't give up hope", he said. "There is no Eleanor". Even my newly cynical brain would not discard this as a sign of obvious flirting. I didn't get why Grayson would suddenly be interested. "I think I'm going to get some air", I said aloud now. None of the others had even budged from their positions, they hadn't noticed how long Grayson and I weren't with them, they were entirely too busy with their own games. "I think I'll accompany you", Grayson quipped. Olive looked up at me, her ears perking up as she got up from her seat. I could sense she wanted to talk to me so I signalled to Grayson that I'd join him in a second.

"What are you doing Esme? He dated Zara remember and you don't want to go through what you felt with Grayson from before do you?", she hissed under her breath. I shook my head disbelievingly and squirmed out of her grip. "You don't know me, Olive, I'm not the same person anymore so you can't stop me", I said coldly. I didn't know the reason behind my frigid manner towards her but something just bothered me about her presence ever since Patrick's party last year.

I rushed to the balcony where I found Grayson standing, bending over the rail. He looked peaceful. He turned when he saw me and I desperately tried to ignore the jolts that occurred in my stomach as he turned his undoubtedly handsome face, keeping his eyes concentrated on mine.

I hadn't had any intimacy since Aaron so it was natural that my body craved it. Abilonians were always too afraid of me to fraternise but Grayson was never afraid of me.

We were standing extremely close. His hands grazed my waist, slowly taking hold of it. My hair was flying out behind me in the wind but all I could feel was his presence. "Esme", he sighed. I waited for him to back out of whatever moment this was. I had always felt so intensely for Grayson that now that whatever I had imagined was finally happening, it was hard to take it all in. We were both guarded yet expressive about each other. It's what I liked about him most, he kept his strength as a mechanism because he had obviously dealt with great deals of pain in his life even if they weren't as unbarred as mine.

I clasped my arms behind his neck waiting for him to talk. "I'm sorry I made the wrong choice back then. It was always you for me, we were just so similar in the most vulnerable way possible that I was afraid. Afraid you would see me for who I am". He rested his forehead against mine. A voice screamed inside my head telling me that this was one of the biggest mistakes I was making but I didn't care. I wasn't in the asylum anymore and I didn't have to evaluate my life. "That's what makes it great Grayson", I whispered. "We can turn our guard into vulnerability to be even stronger". I forgot Grayson had indomitable will too. "We're both evil because we have to be to save us and the world around us". I used to hate being thought of as a monster for what I did to Kipsy City but right now I felt so lucky I lived through that because it assisted this moment with Grayson. One that I wanted to last forever,

Grayson's grip around my waits got even tighter. "Esmerliah, it's things like this that make me question my idiocy for not choosing you every day so I'm not wasting even a second", he said fervently. "What matters is the present, not the past", I said shyly as he leaned in and met my lips with such force yet gentleness that the whole world spun around me. "Sometimes you need the past to make the present work", he murmured against my lips. I kissed him back, running my fingers through his hair as he trailed his mouth down to my collarbone. There was a different voice screaming in my head now but this one wasn't a caviller.

A shout brought both of us back to our senses as we pulled away and looked around us frantically, still holding each other. Levian and Patrick arrived in the doorway but Patrick was looking in the opposite direction pointing outside the window facing the balcony we were in. I looked up at the sky and saw a dark fog clouding it. It was unusual, menacing even. Static sounds echoed through it, making the house shake. I let go of Grayson suddenly when I noticed Levian's downcast expression of disbelief as he looked at us. Pitiful thing, he looked like he saw a ghost and it was quite comical that Patrick was oblivious to the obvious. My word, Patrick's parties sure did cause spectacles although I couldn't argue I enjoyed this one. "You guys should come to the living room", Levian said stoically and walked away and Patrick confused by Levian's harshness pulled us both. "Yeah, the sky is exploding outside, we need to be safe", he screamed and almost toppled over his own feet as he pulled us.

I grinned at Grayson who returned my smile as he pinched my hand playfully. My stomach was exploding inside and I couldn't stop smiling. Everyone was standing up in the living room looking outside the window as Zara switched the television on to see the news. Levian still looked shocked, his mouth almost in a pout as if he were exploding on the inside. At least this time, it wasn't me causing the explosion. I looked outside the window, inspecting the occurrence. It seemed atypical. It may be time to call Betty Harbour back for help. I wasn't prepared to battle whatever was out there on my own…

CHAPTER 16

The Game

The sky that had been gleaming with light at Salt Lake had darkened considerably, and the static sounds that echoed against the clouds increased their volume every minute. It boomed louder and louder, growing more ominous every second. It wasn't normal thunder but almost as the thought crossed my head, the rain started pouring heavily. "The weather is awful, that's what climate change does to you", Patrick said disregarding the static sounds. "Should there be static of that sort?", Zara inquired. It might have been the smartest thing I had ever heard her say because thunder as I knew it didn't produce static that mysterious, nor did it bear the convention of rain that seemed as superficial as a cloud seeding system in a lab. Something seemed terribly wrong but I couldn't comprehend its matter.

I rushed outside, ignoring the calls of both Grayson and Levian as the sky turned a deep, dark shade of blue that looked as murky as laundry washing water. Drops of rain pattered on my face violently and heavily as if they were trying to beat me with each second. I took advantage of the drops that filled my hands with enough power and I shot golden jets of light everywhere and propelled myself upwards to get a closer look at the sky. Never having tried defeating gravity before, this was incredulous. A light bubble formed around me like back in the water when Betty took me to Kipsy City through the lake, lifting me higher and higher as I forced myself to rise. I blinked as the shadow of a shape appeared in the sky for a perfect second but I could have been mistaken.

My head was swarming with screaming voices and I doubted it was just my friends below yelling at me to come down. They looked perplexed, and worried out of their wits but still shied away from the mysterious phenomenon that was taking place. I thrust one hand forward and sent a blast of light into the sky trying to attack whatever was out there and this seemed to only outrage the thunder as the voices in my head grew louder, screaming and demeaning me in every such way. They were the same voices I had in the asylum but this time they were forced into my head. Of course, water having memory could only mean one thing, A nefarious smothered laugh confirmed my suspicion as the shadow finally emerged and I gasped, still maintaining my golden bubble. The repugnant face of Mrs. Hallow flashed across the sky, the outline of a massive cloud projecting her clear, cruel mouth as it boomed. "If you want Kipsy City to remain unharmed and its people, living inside the damage or on the outskirts of it, you will cooperate". Her voice rang out as distasteful and horrid as I remembered.

"The federation has fallen", I screamed. "Your experiments won't work on the people anymore. There are no more innocent people created as monsters to instil fear in the city. No more ethical designer babies made to control the people or make them mindless drones of your totalitarian rule. No more murders to make the federation powerful, your rein is over". I was trembling with emotion.

The Hallows had done enough to the people and I couldn't bear any more people getting hurt. I shot another blast of light towards Mrs. Hallows's face but it deflected. Of course, this was some hologram water projecting, the Harbor Federation had dug deep in their research of water magic and genetically modified humans.

"No sweetheart Esmerliah, nice to see you alive again", Mrs. Hallows smirked. "Controlling your powers huh? You've finally acquired that skill that would have made you very useful to us years ago but instead, you chose to be a rotting failure with that twerp of a woman", she snarled. My face turned red with rage; she was not going to insult Aunt Brie like that. I groaned, Aunt Brie and I had no communication since and if this message was ringing through, it meant Betty was also getting it and Brie would see it.

"I'm not afraid of you", I said instead calmly. "The federation is no more and the people are safe to live life as they can. I'm not the monster and neither is anyone you made out to be. You're the real enemy". Mrs. Hallows face switched out to show a live broadcast of what was happening in Kipsy City. Officers in white and blue suits were rampaging around the ruins of the city and taking the poor city folk outside their houses and injecting serums into them. Children were screaming and crying as some men tried to fight back but the Harbor Federation folk were much too strong and one by one, every person was injected. "Esmerliah, we were in hideout for over two years to perfect our next plan", Mrs. Hallows continued to speak as I watched mortified. "When we thought you were dead, we knew we had no other shot at controlling the people so we perfected our game that we are ready to announce, the same day you appear back. Now thanks to you, your new city is a part of this" I doubled over in disbelief as the footage changed to show Abilo, the confused people screaming as the same Harbor officers injected serums into them. An image of Betty throwing in waves of water and herself as different shapes to fight them back appeared and I saw Ambrosia kicking up her hooves. Aunt Brie was behind Betty, timid but helpful as she ushered people to safety. I was beside myself with rage as an officer grabbed her and injected the serum into her forearm.

"LET HER GO", I growled. "IF YOU HURT HER, I'LL KILL YOU, I'LL BURN YOU ALIVE". I was in hysterics. Every thought that popped into my head right now was about attacking Mrs. Hallow right here and right now. Golden burst of light shot out of me generously, filling the sky up as the sky shone gold, covering the footage. Hot tears shot down my cheeks and I continued my outburst. I had to kill her. I needed to kill her. I wanted her and Gregnitch dead and every single one of those officers who grabbed Aunt Brie and the citizens flogged until they begged for mercy. Mrs. Hallow should be tormented for the years of torture, she has given people. "There is one way you can stop the citizens of Kipsy and Abilo from becoming mindless drones and that is if you play the game alongside those fifteen others of course who show indifference to the serum since you are already resilient to it and will be an Indifferent", Mrs. Hallows now said with a trace of amusement. I execrated how vindictive she was and I needed to stop her and the federation. "What game?", I asked, my eyes shining with golden light, my entire body weaponized and ready to attack.

"Snakes & Ladders", she replied. "If you win, we'll be able to extract enough of your power and satisfy the last bit of our experiment and then we'll never bother you or anyone else again as soon as we have what we need, I promise". The video was replaced again with a board of the game. I raised my eyebrows in disbelief. The children's game? This woman was more cuckoo than I thought. Mrs. Hallows began speaking again. "Sixteen of the Indifferents who cannot submit to the federation's power. As in, the serum has a water base that has a voice that forces the person to obey the rules instructed by us- the federation to keep control and peace in the city. If a person's genetic code doesn't align with the base, they can stop the voice and rebel as Vigilante's which happened years ago and they almost destroyed the federation.". I knew she was talking about Betty. Betty had been one of those vigilante's and she was also an Indifferent now which meant she was going to be in the game. "What happens in the game? What if an Indifferent doesn't want to participate?", I asked, my voice hardening. "The game is simple; you will be trying to find an exit using ladders in an arena. If you are bitten by enough snakes or if you finish last or in the last ranks, you will be eliminated. As in the snakes would already do the eliminating for you. There are recovery sweets laid out in the arena but they don't have enough power if you're bitten more than thrice", she replied. "If an Indifferent wants to disobey the federation and not play the game despite being an Indifferent, they'll be shot right there on spot. If there are more Indifferents than the sixteen we predicted, the remainder will either be kept for genetic surveillance or shot on spot too. We can't have more radicals in the city.

This is the only way we can keep control and prosperity". Mrs. Hallows face vanished and the sky returned to its bright colour.

I let myself back down to the ground and fell with a thud. Grayson helped me up, pulling me to my feet. Everyone was standing outside now staring at me. "Let's go inside, Salt Lake isn't exempt from the game so there will be officers here any minute", I said and everyone nodded. Marshall locked and bolted the door as Patrick turned on the news. Both Abilo & Kipsy City must have had the same announcement as the news reported the happenings and showed similar pictures of officers injecting serums into the citizens. "You're not going to actually play the game, are you? It's dangerous and you could be killed by those genetically engineered snakes", Zara whined. I grimaced at the thoughts; I never had a particular fancy for snakes but I had made up my mind. "I have to play and either way if I refuse, they'll only shoot me. If I win, I can use whatever is at the end and stop the federation forever and its control. I need to protect my aunt and all of you guys", I said as Olive and Patrick put their arms around me. Everyone followed suit and joined in for a group hug. "What if one of us is an Indifferent?", Patrick questioned breaking himself apart from the hug. "Not everyone's genetic code can match their serums". Before I had time to register that, the door suddenly was broken down as the Harbor Federation officers in blue and white armour, stormed in, their needles out.

Levian pushed everyone out of the way, trying to shield them from the officers and I instinctively took a glass and threw water up in the air, unleashing another force of golden light at them. I hadn't thought about Patrick's question. It seemed likely that one of our friends could be an Indifferent so I needed to stop them from getting injected if I could, especially since everyone's names would be available from the injection as each person in Kipsy City especially already had their DNA listed in their federation records. One officer deflected it with a shield he quickly grabbed from his pocket and hit me in the head with it causing me to tumble to the ground squirming. The shield seemed to have a very effective shocker as well. Zara and Olive shrieked as two officers roughly pinned them across the wall and injected them. If Zara became an Indifferent, it would be miserable for her considering she would never be able to go to NYU. I couldn't let any of them be in the game.

An officer injected his needle into my forearm last after everyone else was injected and I felt the sensation of my blood rushing in the wrong direction as I momentarily felt lightheaded. My eyes blurred over as I could make out the shape of a drone outside the window. The federation seemed desperate to record everything they did. I must have passed out for a solid twenty minutes because I woke up to the sky being a little darker than it last was, everyone else seemed as ruffled as I was as they sat up. Zara was hugging her knees. "Patrick, I don't think you should ever host parties again, something awful always happens", she said accusingly. We all exchanged glances at this and burst out laughing. It was only Zara who could make a moment seem so normal and fish out an issue this tiny. Levian was staring at me in concern but a little part of my brain said he was still thinking about Grayson kissing me. I smiled at him which he didn't return but hugged me tightly.

“I wish you weren’t going back in the game; I can’t lose you again”, he said. “You won’t lose me don’t worry”, I whispered patting his back. “Promise me you’ll take care of them?”. He nodded in response and Grayson pulled me out of the room. He cupped my face in his hands, looking at me straight in the eyes, my soul always was lit into flames when I gazed into his eyes. He made his words very candid. “Esme, you’re the strongest girl I know and I want as much of you that I can get before you need to go play this game. I’m not going to leave you”. I nodded a yes and pressed my lips against his again, overwhelmed with emotion for the second time today but this was the better kind. Whatever was to come our way, it would come tomorrow but for now, this was the moment I wanted and nobody could ruin it. All I wanted to feel was Grayson and it felt so right having our lips meshed, holding each other as if we would never let go. Sometimes all I wanted was to be just Esme and not Esmerliah…

CHAPTER 17

Snakes & Ladders

The results were being announced of who the unlucky Indifferents were. I was actively staying over at Levian's house back in Kipsy City waiting to hear the news. On the occasion of both of his parent's demises, it was easier for me to reside with him without suspicion or calling my parents which I doubt Aunt Brie would be too happy with either. My hatred towards the Hallows had increased tenfold, there wasn't any fear anymore and the goal was simple. I had to take down the federation once and for all and play their dirty game and ensure everyone was as safe as I could afford them to be.

Levian had turned the news on and we listened to who the sixteen genetically antagonistic individuals were. It was no surprise to me when I heard the news report call out my name as first. "Esmerliah Hallows an Indifferent to be available for the game". It was wretched and possibly far beyond stupid but I had made up my mind. Levian brewed some coffee for me as I watched intently to know the rest of the participants. "Betty Harbor", the report continued. I grinned; she wasn't going to like that the least bit. The report continued on for a few names until I felt my stomach lurch as my heart dropped down to my sandals. "Grayson Cohen... Brie Larson" I felt like I was going to throw up. Grayson in the game with me sounded temptingly comforting but it was at a manganous risk and Aunt Brie? Maybe it was a different Brie and I never even knew she had a surname. It sounded vaguely familiar but my mind could not focus on the whereabouts of my aunt's last name. I gasped a few more times as Levian's name was called out and Olive's as well as a few people I had known back when I was trapped with the Hallows.

"Levian, it's too dangerous for you guys, I had no idea any of y'all would be Indifferents", I said clutching at Levian's hands hysterically. "Please Levian, let me get you guys to safety, we don't even know anything about this game!" I didn't understand why Levian looked rather cross at my eagerness of having him safe. He laid down his coffee cup with a slam on his kitchen counter. "You want to be alone with Grayson again, don't you?", he asked in the most accusatory tone anyone had ever spoken to me in. I turned around to face him, a little too haughtily. "Levian, I'm genuinely worried for all three of you and my aunt whilst I have a mission to complete so, please don't turn your *evident* jealousy around to me". An indignant spark in Levian's eyes caused me to shut up and he sat down on the floor, burying his head into his hands without a word. I had never seen him cry before and I realised he was afraid. He had no powers; he was frightened of his end after the game and I longed to guarantee him some protection but I knew I couldn't do that.

I sat down beside him, trying to comfort him as well as I could. "Levian, I'm sorry, I didn't mean that, I'll be right beside you all the time, okay? I promise". I stroked his hair as he rested his head against my chest, his arms wrapped around me tightly. He looked up at me and I was aghast to see tears pouring down his cheeks rapidly. Vulnerability on another person's face was always taxing to look at. It peaked my anxiety but I continued being as comforting as I possibly could. "I'm sorry Esme, it's just that after my parents died, it's been really hard. After everything that has happened and I just couldn't risk losing you too. Especially as I already thought I lost you once and it's just too soon to lose you". I felt evil beyond reason. Despite Grayson and I playfully arguing about who's eviler between the two of us, it didn't feel like quite so much an accomplishment now as I remembered Grayson muttering the same words to me about not wanting to lose me. It made me blush with guilt as I couldn't shake off the feeling that Grayson's words had caused more excitement and warmth to unfurl in my stomach while Levian's only made me feel sorry for him. It didn't help that he was actually worried about losing me again rather than his own uneventful fate. "You won't I promise Levian", I say unsure of myself as my voice barely rose above a whisper.

"Now we should get prepared before the federation guards come pick us up and take us to whatever arena the game is set in", I added and we both got dressed and prepared for whatever the Hallows had in store for us.

* * *

The rest of the day before we arrived at the game felt like a blur but here, we all were, our arms being dragged out by the guards as I stood with the other Indifferents in front of a giant candy-themed board that had an image of a snake and ladder on it. We were in a dome-shaped building which meant as we entered, we would be in the arena.

My stomach did a backflip as I watched Gregnitch and Mrs. Hallows arrive with some other federation members. They were behind a large glass wall and a screen that would apparently show us the rules. When I met Betty again, she seemed downcast but her most human version of herself with her red hair cascading down her shoulder, her face pointed and sleek as her slender figure ushered me towards Aunt Brie. I hugged her tightly when I saw her, she didn't mention me sneaking out and all we exchanged was how much we loved each other and wished each other good luck. Grayson and Levian stayed close by me the whole time while Olive was at a close distance to us not wanting to interrupt our little reunion and I was glad she wasn't with us. A wicked part of me even hoped for a fraction of a second that she would not be a winning member of the game. It's wrong to consider your once upon a time best friend with such animosity that you wish implemented murder on them but sometimes as a person, you feel yourself far beyond emotional wreckage to bother much about your most heinous thoughts.

Gregnitch explained the game and I linked my fingers with Grayson who was scanning the crowd for all the other Indifferents. "All of you here have consented to play due to being genetically ignorant of our code and control which means you will have to win if you want to continue on with your lives. In other words, you will each have a number of yards you can cross before you are attacked by snakes and if and when you are, you will be thrown down a number of yards by a mechanical staircase. When you cross a few yards, you can use your personal dice to roll a number every hour to uncover a ladder. If the dice lands at an even number, you'll find a ladder, if it lands at odd, you won't. The fewer players left in the game, the more chances you have at winning. The first three players to finish the game and reach the end will be able to get out of the game as the winners while the rest will, unfortunately, perish alongside their genetic malfunction. If you choose to resign from the game now, keep in mind you will be shot on spot considering your disobedience in even *being* an Indifferent".

I felt a chill run down my spine as goosebumps filled my arms and legs. I had to win somehow but I hadn't even considered staying alive. I looked at my aunt, Betty, Levian, Grayson and even Olive. I never understood the questionable resentment I had towards Olive after Patrick's birthday almost two years ago but I knew it was enough to not think about her being one of the three winners or survivors which made more sense. Two other people but myself? I tried hard not to think of the possible combinations of the two other people I wanted to live with the most when I had four of them with me. I was saved from the rumination by Betty's angry mumbling. "They just want more people to control so they're trying to eliminate those who don't follow them".

Each Indifferent looked furious but they were forced into the arena which appeared to be level woods with some mechanical steps that would lift them up and down eventually. "Okay it's snakes and ladders which means we have to get to the end safely", I chimed in with Grayson who said the last part of the sentence with me. I looked at him and smiled. A part of me was delighted he was here with me despite the thought of his parents worrying and our friends watching the game on live television as they prayed, they didn't find their friends dead later.

Olive was fearfully clinging on to Levian and Aunt Brie and Betty who seemed to get along famously now walked through the woods with us as we explored ways to navigate to the end. As a child, I had played Snakes and Ladders before which is why this game confused me as much as it did. We were walking in the woods for about twenty minutes, locating our dice on almost every patch of land but failing to land on an even number to find a ladder when a cry from Olive caught my attention. Levian was bending over trying to help her as she was sitting on the ground biting her lip in fear. Olive was always so sheepish, pity-seeking that it was almost abstruse to unmask her pain as a cry for sympathy. "What happened?", I asked a little more callously than I desired.

"A snake bit her, it was a genetically modified one and she needs something", Levian answered. I felt a twinge of jealousy seeing Levian care for Olive as much as he did which subsided once Grayson slipped his hand around my waist. "How did the snake suddenly appear, we were all here together?", Aunt Brie asked Levian and I smiled. Brie's candidness always asked the right questions. "Brie, I saw someone push her in that direction and this girlie rolled right into the snake's sight, I think they're tryna get playas eliminated", Betty said and I tried not to think about this. Her theory was proven right when the sounds of more yell out in the woods greeted us as it became apparent that the other Indifferents were killing each other in order to win and get out of the game quicker. I wondered if that was going to happen to us since only three could get out or if we would just be poisoned by the snakes taking us on by surprise. I used the drops of water I could find to accentuate my golden light that I blasted across the yard. My dice turned to an even number just then revealing a ladder -looking object that placed itself under me taking me several yards above the land I was just on. I looked around dazed and pulled onto Grayson's sleeve with me dragging him along as Aunt Brie waved at me.

"We'll see you soon Esme darling, I'm giving some snake medicine to Olive, I tucked some in your jeans pockets too some time ago so you'll be safe and I trust Betty will come and help you with some more of it if you need it", Brie called out to me as she leaned over to help Olive as Levian aided her. He did not turn to talk to me, he was so intent on helping Olive while Betty waved wildly. If Levian didn't live, I would loathe Olive for the rest of my life for being the reason I never had a last glance at my best friend. Grayson held my hand tightly as he kissed me with such force that I almost toppled backwards. "We're in this together and we're winning this Esme, I love you alright? No matter what", he said earnestly. "I love you too Grayson, I always have", I replied.

One Indifferent held a circle around my neck, trying to stab me with his knife as Grayson pulled him off me and hit his head across a tree, beating him up before he put his arms protectively around me. The knife had grazed Grayson's shoulder during his fight and after gasping for several bouts of air, I sent out blasts of golden light shaped like daggers towards the Indifferents who continued trying to bombard us with knives.

Luckily, a snake bit two of them and they were fortunately distracted as Grayson's dice landed on an even number and we rose up another ladder that I almost didn't get on if it weren't for Grayson's good hand pulling me up. I tended to his cut using my magic, healing him with my golden water powers. "You're my angel", he said pulling me towards him as we approached a higher level of yarding. "And you're my devil", I said jokingly as he kissed me again, this time with more desire. We walked onto the new bit of yarding and we stopped in our tracks. I felt my pulse stop and felt like throwing up again at the sight. Olive was leaning over Aunt Brie, trying to feed her Brie's own medicine for snake poison while Brie was lying down straight on her back, blood flowing from her stomach. I ran to her, getting covered in her blood myself but I didn't care. I felt paralysed as a voice screamed inside my head again in torment. "Three snakes bit her at the same time, some Indifferents pushed her towards the third one and I had to make sure I didn't die first", Olive said apologetically but I was beside myself.

"Will she be alright? Why is she bleeding so much? WHY IS THE MEDICINE NOT WORKING?". My volume increased with all the questions I fired towards Olive. I despised her for being so selfish especially after my dear sweet aunt saved her life. Aunt Brie opened her eyes to a slit and looked at me directly. "Esme, it's okay you have no choice now", she said. "I'll be fine but you need to go and stop the federation by winning". Her weak voice was such a change from the confident one almost five minutes ago. Tears poured down my cheeks. "Brie I'm so sorry, I should have never gone down to the lake when you told me not to in the first place and we would have continued being happy together. I'm so sorry, I'm so stupid!", I sobbed. Grayson was rubbing my back reassuringly. Brie held my hand with all her energy. "Esme, this has always been your life and I should have never allowed you to forget about it when you needed to deal with it however hard it was. I love you, you're my only family and always will be and when you win this game and stop the Hallows, I will forever be proud of you even if I don't recover from the bites. I knew it the moment Betty walked in the door, the moment I saw your note on the kitchen table. No, the moment you went down to the lake and the police fetched you back. In fact, I knew it the moment you begged to get your memory wiped out properly and the moment you manifested that little ball of energy in a glass when you saw me, a stranger in your house at 11 while trying to bear the paint he Hallows were going to inflict upon you yet again".

Her little speech seemed to knock the wind out of her as she remained silent trying to breathe what I tried not to think would be her last few breaths. I wasn't good at last words, what could I tell her that I wouldn't regret failing to do later? "Brie, I love you, I love how you never treat me as a child and use appropriate vocabulary with me". This was embarrassing but I never did voice this out loud to my aunt. She smiled at me holding my hand until her eyes turned glassy and her blood stopped spilling. Grayson pulled me and I knew it was time to go as I glared at Olive with incomprehensible incandescence. "You'll play for this Olive, and after she saved your *life*? You will pay for this", I shrieked. I held her fully responsible and didn't hear her justification as tears streamed down her cheeks. Why was *she* crying? I always knew I hated her; I really hope she didn't make it out now, she didn't deserve to. "Where's Levian and Betty?", Grayson asked me. He hadn't lifted his hands off me yet afraid I'd do something rash. I adored the protectiveness he had for me. I wondered the same as more alarm passed through me as there weren't already enough emotions. Where had Olive left Levian and Betty? I trusted Betty enough to keep him safe with her powers but she did have a selfish streak. "Let's try to find them", I said trying my best to continue surviving until Grayson and I emerged as winners. I flinched as I saw a snake bite into another Indifferent praying it wasn't Levian or Betty. My only prayer to God was for them to be safe and alive… How I wish Snakes and Ladders was never a popular board game. I never expected it to cost me the loss of someone I loved so dearly that it physically hurt to see their loss occur right before my eyes.

CHAPTER 18

The Real Snakes & The Real Ladders

As it turned out, Grayson and I couldn't go down levels the same way we went up yards through the mechanical ladders so we had to search for Betty and Levian on our own level. There was no more water we could spare to use up for me to try to connect with Betty through our water portals and Grayson's phone had been taken from him before the game began. I was already a grieving mess by the time we gave up trying to search for them and sank down leaning against a large oak tree as we simultaneously kept watch for any snakes.

I was exhausted, sleep had become a common stranger and the dark circles under my eyes started filling up more space on my face than I could care for. My eyes burned with my sinuses and tears rapidly plopped down on the hem of my shirt I borrowed from Levian every two minutes. I officially cried out and it hurt too much to shed more tears.

Three fat tears just dropped from my eyes and I caught them in the palm of my hand feeling the tingle of a golden light spark. "You're starting to need less and less water to do that", Grayson pointed out, kissing the side of my head gently as I shut my eyes and imagined what my Aunt Brie would look like in heaven. A golden angel figurine with her face and a medicine bottle replaced the tears in my outstretched hand and I gave it to Levian. He was right, I had gained so much control over my magic that I required less and less water to obtain it now, quite different from that eleven-year-old child who could only unleash her magic with blasts unknowing of its power. "I think it's the understanding that makes me better at it", I said. "Memorizing the feel of the golden light and imagining just what I want, controlling my emotions in tentative amounts so it doesn't go all frantic".

Grayson laced his fingers in mine as the golden light from it surrounded them. "Make me something else that isn't the Eleanor chain you made back at Patrick's house", he said in a commanding voice to which I laughed. "I could make you a figurine of Zara, I'm getting quite good at them you know", I said cheekily and ducked as Grayson clutched his face in mock horror. "Okay, how about you make one of Aaron or that awful HB", he retorted and I glared at him before the two of us burst out laughing. I twirled my fingers up as I imagined the three, creating dancing models of Zara, Aaron and HB floating in the air for three seconds before they disappeared. "Woah, Aaron and HB looked so much younger in that", Grayson commented and I shrugged. "It's what I remember from the rotating Liah".

I buried my head in Grayson's chest as he started to get up hesitantly. "I hear something Esme", he said clenching his fists together. All at once, three snakes darted at us, one folding itself around Grayson, snaking its forked tongue out at his face, teasing which place it was about to bite him in. They were hideous, long-tailed creatures of purple and green, with huge eyes rancid eyes that popped out of their sockets. Grayson was failing to lung out of the snake's grip as one wrapped itself around me menacingly and I struggled to breathe. The most horrifying images flashed before my face of the Hallows murdering each and every single person in the city, the image of Aunt Brie dying in my arms and I couldn't tune the hair-rising hum that was constantly playing in my ear. My hands weren't free enough to create any blasts which served as a problem. My eyes shone with golden light, stupefying the snake holding Grayson that sank dead to the floor and he rushed towards me just as I felt the snake's tongue graze my neck.

This was the end; I hadn't won and I wasn't going to be able to stop the Hallows now and die instead. Pain surged through my body, my blood felt like it was on fire, and my face felt like it had swollen lumps mounting everyone and every part of my body hurt. Even my hair hurt! I felt the snake release me as the shadow of Grayson ran over to me and a cool female voice and shout were the last things I could hear faintly before everything blurred out and went blank.

"Girlie, ya awake?" I cautiously opened my eyes to Betty leaning over me, her legs liquid like but her body still intact and human. I got up and looked around me. I was in a bubble similar to the one in the lake I first saw Betty in. "Am I dreaming?", I croaked, clearing my throat multiple times. "Aren't ya one for ugly sounds? And no dearie, ya aren't dreaming but apparently, when you're injected with snake poison, your body unleashes stored water from your magic", Betty responded. "What about everyone else, won't they drown if we're still in the game?", I asked trying my best to stand up but my hands were too numb to work. "I used Brie's medicine to get rid of your cut", Betty pointed at the gash in my neck, ignoring my question.

Typical of Aunt Brie to make sure everyone was safe first. The remnants of her potion were used up by Betty who I noticed had several cuts across her legs. "You were bitten by four snakes? I'm surprised the medicine even helped you". I couldn't subdue my curiosity even with the knowledge of Betty being a long-timed survivor, if anyone could win the game, it would be her. "Ehh, it's about the will to survive and I fought off the snakes before they sank their stupid Hallow- made teeth in me too far", she replied casually.

"Ohh, I helped your friends climb onto that ledge", Betty said directing me towards a rock on the surface of the lake. Grayson must have gotten another even number and lifted above surface level. "I covered all these levels with water?", I asked Betty again who nodded chuckling. "Yeah, ya killed like everyone below, it was hysterical how many Indifferents are dead without getting bitten". I never fully understood Betty's sense of humour despite my fascination with it but my allure was replaced by mortification. I gritted my teeth; I was done getting played by the Hallows in their multiple games and this time I meant it to end.

I let go of the bubble with my hands, and swung my hands around until the water disappeared and Betty and I were standing on land, Betty sitting abruptly due to the absence of the warning I gave her to return to human legs. "Hey watch out!", she exclaimed crossly before shifting into human form again. I looked at her solemnly, an idea forming in my mind. “Betty, I think you should be the first to exit the game”, I said confidently as she looked at me bemused.

“I’d still come in second of course”, I clarified. “But you’d be the one to stop the Hallows and everything the federation made you do and the enemy they made you would be a warrior who did what’s right”. I had never been surer of my decision. Betty may be feared by dozens for all the people she had murdered but Grayson was right, it was the past and while it still connected with the present, I knew Betty as the girl who took great care to help me out by telling my loved one, I was safe and protected her until she couldn’t. She rescued me at the lake, sheltered my confusion and guarded me as I tried to unravel my own past. Most of all, she never judged me for the damage I created but instead *actually* empathised with it and saved me from imminent death which boosted my confidence in who I was. She was like a ladder, she lifted me up levels even at my oddest numbers. My aunt liked her enough as a companion and trusted her enough with her guarded, beloved niece so I would slip my dead aunt’s faith into my own as I trusted my fellow water fugitive with my life and the future of Kipsy City and Abilo. It’s what she deserved nonetheless.

Her quizzical look was enough to make me burst out laughing and I pulled her into a sudden and awkward hug that she only returned after two minutes of confusion. “Betty, I trust you, Brie trusted you and you’ve been a friend to me, a saviour and that’s more than anyone’s ever been to me in my life after Brie", I said earnestly, my voice going quiet as I remembered Brie. Betty's resplendent face blushed with happiness and I was glad to see how touched she was by my words. It's funny how people mature, I always considered Olive to be my best friend in the past yet she was the one I could trust the least, who let her selfishness betray me several times and the person who even saved her life and while she would forever fill me up with rage, Betty was the one who righted that fury into a broad smile. Betty Harbour had successfully proved to be an effective best friend, a ladder much like Levian had been. They lifted me up at both odd and even rolls and that's how I knew I was lucky enough and I loved Betty dearly for it. She was different and she was in no manner a replacement for Olive, she was too unique for that but she was an addition I could not exist without and she was the perfect motive to stop the Hallows and the federation who made her suffer as much as it made me. "Betty you're my best friend, let's get out of this game", I said and she grinned another broad grin as she rolled her dice to an even number and the platform beneath us rumbled to take us up.

The sight of Levian and Grayson fighting two Indifferents with knives grasped our attention as I tried to bash my golden light onto them. It didn't work, I must have used up all my energy getting better and now the light failed me. An Indifferent rushed towards me advantageously aiming his knife at my face, the look of despair on his ragged face intriguing me. I could never forget that look, the urgency to survive reminded me a lot of my own in the Liah and it was unfortunate the federation had done this to people. I was filled with anger again; control was all the Hallows desired and it had been brought down to torture just to control the people. I tried to fend off the Indifferent with my bare hands when Betty torpedoed his attack, front rolling onto him, plucking the knife out of his surprised fist before calmly yet violently stabbing it right in the centre of his chest. The look of despair was fixed on his face as he fell to the ground, his eyes wide open, tainted with spatters of blood that erupted from his bleeding chest.

Nobody got a word in when Betty placidly attacked the second Indifferent in the same manner, pulling out the gaping knife from the first Indifferent' s chest, her expression still tightened into a grin as she kicked the second Indifferent over, held him up by his throat and stabbed him thrice. Once in the stomach, once a little above and finally his neck after which he fell, his eyes already shut accepting his fate on the first stab. Levian, Grayson and I watched frozen as Betty once more pulled the knife out aiming for Grayson whose usually brave eyes sparkled with fear.

"Betty Betty, stop", I said as she kept down the knife and laughed at Grayson's uneasy expression. "Well, they are all done now, let's get out of the game, three people is all we need and I don't think anyone is left", she announced as we all spun our dice at the same time. Luck was back on our side as they all turned even and we were lifted up onto the final level.

I slipped my hand back into Grayson's sensing some tension as Levian eyed us in obvious discomfort. I already knew what he was thinking, he had just seen Betty's killing rampage and the game only accepted three winners which meant it was either him, Grayson or me who would have to die. Levian would never want me dead and I was assertive he let himself wish for Grayson's demise. I didn't want to lose either of them and smiled reassuringly at Levian who unknowingly grabbed my shirt sleeve, not wanting to let go of me. I reached out for his hand too and the three of us walked, hand in hand. "We're reaching the end, I see it", Grayson said pulling me to walk faster with him and the four of us quickened our pace, watching out for snakes concurrently.

We reached the last platform before the final level-up when we saw the last person, I wanted to see rolling her dice. "Olive, you're alive", Levian asked happily as he let go of my hand and rushed to hug her. She smiled at him, kissing him on the cheek and I burned in frustration. Olive was too selfish to live but there had to be a choice that was made. "I'm not killing your friend girlie", Betty whispered grimly, reading my expression. "This one's on ya". Olive caught my reverberating stare as she ran to hug me. "Esme, I'm really sorry about your aunt but she was going to die anyway. I want you to live, you're my best friend and I just didn't know how to talk to you when you came back, I wouldn't have gone to the federation back in school a year ago about your explosive, dangerous powers if I wasn't concerned for you so you should know how much I love you", she berated her doleful voice causing plops of blood in my body to move anxiously.

"You got me in the asylum?", I managed to ask. The more I stood in front of Olive, the more I wished her dead in the game. "It was only for your own good Esme, you're my best friend!", she replied and Betty shoved her. "Hey human lady, me and that boy Levian are her best friends because we are actually helping her survive and vice versa", she said pointing the knife at Olive's throat. "Now I wasn't gonna kill you lady, but someone has to go and you've angered me". Betty flashed her teeth smiling. "Goodbye Olive, this is for Brie, my newest friend whose death ya are very much responsible for". I looked away from Olive, I didn't want to witness this. Betty was about to slash the knife across her throat when I heard a thud.

I looked up. Grayson had pushed Betty aside as he took the knife into his own hand and slashed her throat. Olive's screams filled the arena and I stared at him incredulously as he rolled his dice to an even number. His eyes searched mine and he aimed the knife at Levian's face, thrusting it at him with full force before the latter could react. Horror filled me as everything descended too quickly after that. I stepped in front of Levian, the knife nearly missing me and inserting itself into Levian's gaping mouth, it had gone all the way down to his throat and his eyes locked with mine as they closed almost immediately, his blood spilling everywhere. Every voice in my head was screaming now. I felt faint, not registering Grayson's murder yet as I fell to my knees at Levian's blood- spattered, limp body, begging for him to wake up as his blood trickled down my face, arms and legs. I swallowed large amounts of his blood mixed with my tears as I screamed. Betty pushed Grayson off the ladder as she overtook him for the final level to win over him, her instincts catching up with him. They were gone without a word as Grayson's betrayal, his kill and the consequence burst inside me. I felt like I was dying as I kept nudging and screaming for Levian to awaken. Grayson was nothing but a malevolent, guileful snake, much worse than the one who had bitten me. He was my friend who I had fallen in love with and his bite was not one of love's, it was poison to everyone I loved and me. How could I have been so blind? I rested my head across his stomach, not letting go of his hand, ignoring the knife that was still inserted inside his mouth and sobbed and sobbed until I passed out again.

CHAPTER 19

The Winning Indifferent

"Esme come on, we have to go", said the last voice I wanted to hear. How could someone who brought me such comfort just a few minutes ago spur such disdain in me now? "Do not touch me Grayson", I warned, my voice giving away, hoarse from screaming for Levian to wake up. I hadn't moved an inch away from his body. "Betty pushed me down, she's at the top anyway and you and I are the only two people left in the game to leave", he said quietly, attempting to pull me up again. "You killed your own freaking friends Grayson!", I yelled. "You've known them since you were a little kid" …

Grayson slid down beside me, looking directly into Levian's eyes as he turned over his corpse away from me and put his arms around me. I howled from him to leave as I frantically started beating against his chest. Grayson allowed me as he simply placed my head under his chin and stroked my hair before pressing a quick peck on my forehead." I deserved that", he said finally shutting his eyes as he released me from his grasp.

I despised how even after he betrayed me and killed two of our friends, I still longed for his comfort, his presence with me. It was hard to lose that longing for someone when all you remember is wanting them closer to you every second.

"Why did you do it?", I finally asked looking him straight in the eyes. "Levian loved you Esme, he always has and only three Indifferents can leave this game alive", he replied truthfully. "I wasn't going to be the one dead, killing Betty was too overpowered and imagine the victory I could bring if I stopped the Hallows and the Harbor Federation myself". I froze at his words. "

"Yourself?", I repeated unbelievingly. "Myself Esmerliah Hallows, myself", Grayson said in a cold, mocking voice I wasn't acquainted with. His tone sounded anomalous and I could feel my already stunned heart from Levian and Brie's deaths cracking away by its remnants as Grayson continued to speak.

"Your friend Betty is too quick for me, she's much too smart so I'm assuming the federation turned her into some robotic monster which is why I had to figure out another way, causing her impulsiveness to avoid finishing first". The callous expression had replaced the warmth vigour Grayson always radiated. "You can't finish first, you don't have the power to stop the federation and there will be a fight that only Betty and I are equipped to win", I said biting away at my lip anxiously.

Grayson smiled his usual good-natured smile, his intention however anything but magnanimous as he stroked my cheek carelessly, kneeling over to me. I winced at his touch, his betrayal growing larger and larger in my heart. Grayson was the last person I expected to turn over into a power-hungry maniac. It explained why he was an Indifferent at any rate." Esme, you just saw me kill both Olive and Levian within a manner of seconds using one knife. Oh, and speaking of the dead, Olive did not intentionally act cowardly when she left your aunt with the snakes, I had a calling chip I gave her saying we all had one and told her you were dying and needed her help on the other side but you never let her continue with what she had to say so I told her to save it for later and whisked you off, away from her. I just knew that if your aunt died earlier on, you'd be emotional but not enough to ruin your game completely so I saved Levian for the end". This little speech made by him made my cheeks burn with rage. I wanted to throttle him. Olive may have had her faults but all she wanted was to keep me safe. It was too much to process and I did not want to believe Grayson had done all this when I didn't fully understand his motive.

I despised myself even more for the fact that I still wanted to portray Olive as the enemy despite Brie's death not being her fault but Grayon's. Despite her telling Grayson I liked him a year ago because she must have had an instinct that our dating would have been a terrible idea. I knew Olive well enough to understand that and I didn't know why my judgement was so clouded before. The asylum in the rotating Liah *had* been the place that jogged all my other memories back into my head which meant it had some effect on me which unfortunately meant that Olive had been right all along. I sighed out loud. "What did Olive say to you when she told you I possessed feelings for you a year ago?', I asked Grayson evenly. His mouth curved upwards in a smile, he must think I'm foolish to ask such a futile question in a game of life and death where he was clearly going against all odds to win.

"Typical Esme, dying yet you still want to know something so utterly pointless with your persistent little head, can't say I'm still not attracted to it.", he teased flirtingly but now other than sinking more cracks into my heart, his manner only vexed me, it was an affliction that caused me dire agony. "I'm not dying Grayson but do fill me in", I said staidly to which he caused no objection. "Oh, I knew for a while Esme, the way you acted around me told me enough. If you're intuitive, remember I have more than enough of that skill and that's why I'm an Indifferent in the first place. Intuition is what makes us Indifferents, not your ridiculous waterworks. It keeps us questioning the control, sensing something new and the federation doesn't want that which is why I need to stop it once and for all and take control myself", he answered. He fiddled his thumbs absentmindedly, not bothering to answer my question.

"And yes, you and Betty winning means you fight the federation, you fight the Hallows and you make them keep their promise by leaving Kipsy City and Abilo alone forever. The only two places with a perfected memory serum and high-tech genetic machines that can create what you are- a designer baby or perform surgeries far beyond our times. You should know considering you've been involved in all of those things Esme. I used you here to keep myself from winning and I would have left you with those snakes who bit you if it hadn't been for Betty and Levian coming up to help you, Levian was already getting suspicious so he trailed me, he's always kept an eye out for my usually unorthodox political beliefs. So once Betty and you are out of the way and I win, I'd be the only Indifferent but I'd ask the Hallows to give me some of the control as my reward or let them leave if I'm not content enough with it but I wouldn't stop what they have going on, if it weren't for control there would be people killing everyone on the streets just like you did all those years ago Esme. Oh, and don't worry, Levian and Olive could have surgery performed on them by some of the federation's futuristic surgeries, they aren't necessarily dead but we'll see if there's time"

I was aghast. I couldn't let him win and then it hit me. "Olive told you it wasn't a good idea to lead me on, didn't she?', I asked softly, realization dawning on me. "Does it matter?", he replied. I wiped my face clean with my hands, standing up for the first time, ignoring how jelly- like my legs felt. "She told you I was too full of emotion for you to play with my heart if you wanted to keep our friendship going?", I continued asking walking towards him. Grayson folded his arms and nodded. "She did and she was right, you always let emotion get the better of you Esme, you need control and before you couldn't even control it to the extent where your powers would not show everyone what you felt. I cared about you as a friend too much to have you hurt or kill me with your powers when you knew I never meant for anything serious to happen so I continued what I had with Zara.". Grayson was staring right into my eyes as he poured heaps of home truths down them, one by one. He dated Zara, the poor innocent girl who accepted falling in love with one of her close friends, who lived in guilt knowing one of her other friends was suffering as she continued her decision. It was her good fortune when I disappeared and she broke off the relationship.

"Marshall deserves her more Grayson, I hope you know that and your way, *way* eviler than I am and this time I'm not joking around with you", I said profoundly. I remembered the game was being recorded so if any of our other friends were watching this, they'd be both in tears and shock right about now. Grayson knew exactly what I meant, even in his moment of ignoble betrayal and cunningness, he always was that one friend who knew me well, too well for our present and it aggravated me that he looked amused at my outburst and not the least bit hurt by my words. "Esme, don't get me wrong. I do love you and this is nothing personal but it's for the greater good of our cities so you'll thank me later. I don't plan on killing either you or Betty. I was always attracted to you, we always had something and even if I used these last few days to get closer to the federation to enforce my plans, I enjoyed my time with you and I really wish it wasn't ending like this. You are and always will be one of my closest friends, one of the best kissers I've pressed my lips too and one of the boldest girls I could have wickedly humoured banter with and it's what makes you and I the winning Indifferents.".

Grayson stepped closer to me and clasped his hands around mine. "I'll miss you Esme, I hope you don't mind having your memory reset again but I promise this will be the last and this time it'll all seem like it never happened", he said and gently touched his lips to my mouth before he forcefully sat me down, slid his hand around my waist, grabbed my dice and his and rolled an even number and jumped up to the final level as he pulled a giant oxygen mask over his head for some reason. My heart pounded against my chest; his actions were much quicker than his words that kept repeating themselves in my head. I blinked thrice bringing myself back to my present and darted after him seeing Betty and him both make a beeline for the edge of the woods where a large snake -printed exit sign stood.

Grayson threw something out of his jacket pockets that spread gas everywhere in the woods fogging it up. "Betty!", I called out. "Please tell me you made it", I began coughing as the gas got up my nose, my lungs reeling from the burning sensation. "Can't see, where are ya Liah?", Betty called back. That was the first time I had heard her call me that and apparently, the last memory I would have of this day. My voice was suddenly too tired to speak as I pulled myself forward, the empty feeling in my stomach telling me that Grayson had already won and it was over. I felt hungry and thirsty as I tried remembering the last time I ate. "That's funny, I can't remember", I mumbled. I looked behind me expectantly but I couldn't recall why. Was I calling for someone? I lay down on the ground, curling myself into a ball. I hadn't the faintest idea what I was doing in the woods in a place full of silver mist or was it gas? I didn't understand the heaving feelings of grief, anger, iniquity and despair that seemed to be nestling at the bottom of my stomach. "Maybe I have a bad stomach", I told myself as I shut my eyes, preparing to sleep it off until I felt better…

CHAPTER 20

Aftermath

Tiles. White marble tiles on the ceiling… It all seemed too hazy. Where was I? Everything seemed distant even in eyesight. The blur of the tiles, were they even tiles? They seemed clearer as tiles as my eyes opened wider getting accustomed to the colour, the whiteness. I couldn't move, something heavy was holding me back although I doubted, I could make much movement, it was taking me way too much energy to even keep my eyes concentrate on the tiles. I tiled my face downwards to take in the sight of the instruments wrapped around me. My hands were trapped in two metal- clad handcuffs, tied to either side of a large hospital bed. I wondered the reason why they were placed when my body groaned to even lift my head away from the rest of me.

A straw was inserted into my mouth as my saliva encountered the moderately warm pineapple-like the taste of Gatorade. After around three minutes of composure, I was finally able to fix myself in a position where I could visibly see my surroundings- both the setting and the people who illuminated the shadows against the ceiling tiles-. The taste of water after Gatorade filled my throat, quenching the thirst I did not even know existed. Water never tastes better when you desperately long for it. I thought of all the things that made water the most desired thing on the planet. It could be warm or cold according to preference, it brought up your energy levels and you could get rid of it easily from your body.

Water also stored memories… I could not recall where I learnt that from but that stuck in my head long enough for me to recite the most water- themed poem I could think of as I spouted words between sips.

Water

It's a desire you can never release

It lives inside you yet you can never inaugurate it when you need it most

Water is wet and cold but it's also warm and trickly

It's stinging and standoffish

When you're too full of that magical liquid

You could freeze much like its indignant solid state

Drinking water reminds me of things

The things I always forget

It's an immediate refresher

If health and head held hands

Water is a mere sanction

To power, to freedom and to satisfaction of thirst

Water is a license

To live, continue living and to retrieve whatever you lost

Health, head or even power

Water is drowning, it's boiling, it's also freezing but it's my state of matter that chooses

How water treats me

Water is my power

"Always the wild words of a little Socrates, isn't it? Or did you mean actual water?" I stopped reciting and looked up to see a rough face of a stony- eyed woman. I got up frantically in my seat trying to get up but the handcuffs prevented me from getting up. "What are you doing here?", I asked, my voice a mixture of a yelp and a cry. "Sit down Esme, you're having another reaction", says the woman beckoning to the handcuffs as if it was normal for the head of the federation that tortured so many people in my city to just be leaning over my hospital bed. "What reaction?", I snarled. Mrs. Hallows looked undisturbed by my rancour and pointed at the other individuals standing a little away from my bed.

"Your friends are here, maybe you should talk to them", said she walking away before patting the top of my head ignoring the way I flinched at her touch. Levian, Olive and Grayson walked up to me on either side of my bed as I sipped more water from the straw. The memories, while distant, from the previous day's events were still existing within me and it seemed uncanny to have Levian and Olive staring at me with such concern when they both had knives in their throats not even an hour ago. Ridiculous even, it was all the more risible that Grayson having been the murderer and betrayer now stood in the middle of them with falsified concern on his face.

"You used the memory serum, you stole it from the federation, I don't know how but you did!", I yelled accusingly, pointing at Grayson who had the same amused face he did in the game. "Memory serums don't exist in real life Esme", Grayson said placidly. Levian and Olive looked perplexed at my reaction but their expressions bore a reaction that told me they were used to this. "What did you do Grayson", I hissed. "Where's Betty?". "Right here love", Olive said comfortingly placing a rag doll on my lap that eerily resembled what Betty looked like with similar red hair and a slender body with wobbly legs.

"You asked the Hallows for control over Kipsy and Abilo didn't you Grayson? And they gave Levian and Olive the surgeries after you killed them? You had a plan all along just like you wanted. You used me Grayson and I will never forgive you for it". I was beside myself in rage as I tugged against the handcuffs, my adrenaline pumping instant energy in me. "You've had a bad dream Esme, it's okay, I'm right here and you'll be fine. I've got you", Levian said wrapping his arms around my head as I automatically leaned against his stomach. "It's not a dream, it just looks like it because your memories are wiped but mine can't be wiped because water stores memory and I have perfect control over my powers now", I said resisting. "Release me and I'll show you". "Don't release her from the handcuffs Levian", Mrs. Hallows said walking forward, she had been listening to the whole conversation.

"Stay away from me, you're the reason for everything and you took my aunt away from me", I growled at her. "You've been in an accident love", Olive said solicitously moving Levian away so she could stroke my hair. "We had the finals and you were stressed out because you thought you would fail your biology exam and wouldn't be able to get into NYU and study Marine Biology because you love it so much", she said. "You ran after the exam, wanting to be alone and rode off on Patrick's motorbike where you skidded off a bridge into a lake and hit your hands on a few rocks badly so you damaged them", Levian added. I stared at Grayson for a moment who had been decidedly silent. "Okay.", I said a plan forming in my head as I relaxed backwards observing the glance exchanged between Grayson and Mrs. Hallows which was anything but a look of concern for my well-being.

"Grayson, you've been silent for a while, you must know in detail what's happened considering you were there with me the whole time", I said narrowing my eyes. He ran a finger through his thick hair and I sighed. After everything I still couldn't help loving him and his little mannerisms, I hated how I always formed relationships with people who had troubled toxicity as their emblems. Aaron, HB and the one that pained me the most to think about, who was standing in front of me manipulating my whole world. our whole world: Grayson. All for the need for control and I despised the fact that it was essential for people, to be able to live in control because freedom seemed like a threat to them, it was insular thinking, wretched when there was so much depth in people like Grayson and even love.

Grayson plopped down next to my bed in tune with my aggressive thoughts and almost like he read my mind, he replied saying, "We were playing snakes and ladders a minute ago… the board *game* not the weird war game you created in your head that you kept screaming about and then you fell asleep and had another nightmare. You've been like that since your accident and occasionally you'll shift from your lucid state to experiencing hallucinations until you tire yourself and pass out completely". It was abstruse to believe how convincing Grayson could be.

"You have schizophrenia Esme, it's normal for you to behave this way and get confused", Mrs. Hallows said. I wanted to kill her with just a stare. I looked at my hands that were tied up and didn't even bother to muffle my gasp at how ruined they were. There were scars everywhere and they looked burned and bedraggled. They looked like lumps of flesh more than hands. I twisted my hands until I was touching the water with them and winced as my hands burned. I flicked my fingers expecting glowing light to emerge from them but there was nothing. "What did you do to my hands?", I screamed at Mrs. Hallows. "It was the accident Esme, I'm your mother, I would never hurt you". "Let her have her hands back", Levian urged with determination in his voice. I looked at him gratefully, he believed I wasn't going to go into another 'schizophrenic' state and try to kill them all. No that was Grayson's job. Despite Mrs. Hallows protests, he released me from the handcuffs and I wondered how many attacks he believed he saw me have that he was okay to handcuff me. Levian would never try to keep me trapped when he knew how much I hated incarceration, especially after the asylum.

I looked down at my hands, assertive that Grayson's plan had worked and he chose control above everything else but at the same time, I was glad he stuck to his promise and kept Levian and Olive alive. "Oh, Kipsy and Abilo are also a figment of your rustic themes imagine but you knew that already so I guess you're up to date now", Grayson said which doubled my suspicion and annoyance. "Okay I want a word alone with Grayson please", I said and looked directly into Levian's eyes who looked rather reluctant to see me. "Levian, you can come in after ten minutes", I quipped and he looked relieved as he exited the room with Mrs. Hallows and Olive.

We didn't say a thing to each other for a while and Grayson just gazed at me for a few minutes, eyeing me vehemently but also endearingly if I wasn't mistaken. "Tell me the truth, nobody would believe me anyway since I now have schizophrenia apparently thanks to you", I said sweetly, searching his eyes for any falter in his pretence. I found none.

"Esme, I'm sorry I beat you in snakes and ladders and even your doll who you were playing for and you weren't very happy because you're competitive as always. We beat Levian and Olive too and that Captain Marvel figurine that Levian brought with him like the nerd he is", he chuckled as he said that. "Are you serious?". I interrupted aggravated. "Yeah, I mean Brie Larson is hot and all but to have her as your favourite Avenger is pushing it. I'm with you on your choice of Avengers, spiderman is my favourite too especially after you told me I looked like him", he said winking at me. I had the sudden urge to slap him across his face. Grayson knew well enough about the largest crush I had on Tom Holland forever and over a year ago at Patrick's party, I told him about how he resembled him in all physical traits but I was drunk out of my wits and apparently a little too honest.

"You're going to deny kissing me too? You just led me on as Olive told you not to, aren't you?", I said shaking my head as I let the tears engulf all of my sadness and angst towards Grayson. I felt sorrier for Levian, he would not remember a thing related to the tyranny under the non-existing federation thanks to Grayson which meant he probably had no recollection of his parents either who had died at the hands of the hallows, the whole federation. Grayson gave me a look of pity. "Esme, Zara and I just broke up after I caught her cheating with Marshall, I should have known at Patrick's party last year and of course that little celebration at Patrick's house a little while ago when you and I had a moment right before your accident. Zara felt so guilty". I didn't even bother arguing with him and continued crying. I didn't care if I was letting my emotions engulf me once more, it was too much all too soon, after all, I had warred through. My efforts seemed wasted.

"Your eyes are very blue, you look even more radiant when you cry", Grayson said peering at them. He leaned in close to my face until there was only a 5 cm distance between us that I could put a ruler against to measure. My face felt warm suddenly and my eyes blurred out, the only thing I could see was Grayson's beautiful brown eyes that always reminded me of a cow's soft eyes. His beautiful, deceiving eyes were as brown as the snakes that bit people in the game, the snake that bit me. Grayson was the only snake I knew and I was about to get bitten by him again but I was too full of emotion to even resist and I let his lips attach to mine as I felt his tongue tangle my tongue. I fiercely tackled his tongue but he mistook the gesture for romance and now completely pulled himself onto the bed now as he left a trail of kisses down my neck. “I’ve been waiting forever to do this for the first time”, Grayson said grinning down at me.

“Get off her”, Levian said furiously. He was standing in the doorway, holding out a tray of lemon tarts. My favourite as he walked in angrily. Grayson obeyed but didn’t attempt to explain himself. “Oh, come on Lev, I know you’re in love with her but you know as well as I do that, she only reciprocates companionship with you. I’m always in her hallucinations for crying out loud, Esmerliah Hallows and I have something special and I will chance it even after her accident almost destroyed her…”, Grayson said confidently. He landed a kiss on the top of my head which undoubtedly caused Levian’s blood to boil as he flung the tarts at Grayson’s head. I groaned and yelled at them to stop.

“What happened Esme? I’m so sorry, I didn’t mean to”, Levian said hugging me instantly. “No, I just wanted the tarts, y’all can keep fighting but Grayson’s strong Levian, it’s not going to end well and I have seen it before”, I claimed as I reached over to grab a lemon tart. I was just tired at this point. “So, you really want to do this? After he chose Zara over you last year?”, Levian asked me testily. “Lev she’s been in an accident but she knows what she wants and Zara was *last* year and I was just afraid to chance it with Esme because I didn’t want to lose her”, Grayson said his attitude was really annoying and boosting my self-esteem at the same time.

Levian nodded in acknowledgement and got up as Grayson rushed to let him out. “Wait”, I called out. I didn’t know what I was doing but my instincts were pushing me ahead. “Grayson I have one question for you”. “Anything Esme”, he replied eagerly. “Do you think our past should affect our present? Do you see us in the future together? I asked with bated breath, hoping Grayson wouldn’t see through my trap. With his eyes still eyeing the door to let Levian out, he almost immediately answered. “I don’t think your past should affect our present but you seem to think so or you wouldn’t let me kiss…um what does it have to do with anything?”. He looked alarmed; he had fallen for it. I winked at him in glee, there was no possible way Grayson remembered that if he didn’t remember our interaction at Patrick’s house right when the explosions occurred. He wouldn’t have remembered the *real* first time he kissed me which confirmed my memory of Grayson having won the game.

“I think I want to play snakes and ladders again but this time I want only *ladders,* not *snakes*”, I said looking straight at Grayson meaning the insult with all my might. I had made my choice. “Levian, stay with me, it’s in my unwritten future to play a game with you but only on the board. Grayson, you can leave now and next time ask before you kiss me.”, I said enjoying his dismayed expression. He knew what I meant because he obliged half-heartedly as he quietly said, “You’re evil Esme”. “Not more so than you”, I retorted never looking away and I could have sworn I caught a pinprick of a smile on Grayson’s face which was now mostly stoic. “You’ll always be the winning Indifferent Grayson, you beat my intuition”, I added right before he closed the door behind him wistfully staring at me for a second before he left without another word. I believed Grayson loved me enough to give us a chance but he was too desperate for control, too closed off and manipulative to allow a relationship with someone like me who needed support for my emotions and more than a companion- a partner to help me get through these times after my 'accident' because yes that was my current reality and I had to live through it.

"Thank you, Liah,", Levian said to me as he dragged out the board. "You don't want to play again, do you?", I asked laughing as he shook his head with haste. "Oh god no, it's so boring and purely based on luck, there's no strategy in this". I smiled. "Levian, can I ask you something?', I asked. "Anything Esme", he said taking my hand in his with a steady grip as if he was too scared to let me get lost in another schizophrenic attack. "What do you see in the Rotating Liah?". He looked confused as he cautiously chose his next few words. "You mean my dreams, right? I call your dreams the Rotating Liah because you turn your head a lot when you sleep as if you have the wildest things happening to you". I remembered Betty calling me that and I looked at Levian determined to stir some memory at any rate. "Will you tell me about your dreams then?", I beseeched. "Okay I'll go get us some water and then I'll be right back to tell you I promise", he said getting up. The hallows really had been thorough to remember details on Grayson's command. It felt strange having Levian call me Liah. I closed my eyes waiting to digest my new reality as Mrs. Hallows came in with a man who shared her rough, calloused face. I shuddered. "Gregnitch..."

CHAPTER 21

Hopeless Light

Grayson obviously didn't know all the pain he was causing me right by his one egocentric decision. At this point, I couldn't even be *sure* if there was a decision. Grayson could have easily been referring to an amorous 'moment' we had when we discussed the past, present, and future at Patrick's house party and there was high plausibility that I did get into an accident which caused my brain to wheezy. I couldn't understand what was real and what wasn't at this point. I was positive I was in an asylum but that could also just be a therapist trying to get me out of my schizophrenic state that would explain the golden light. It would explain why it always came out of my hands when I regained more control in my body after the accident. The world I just woke up from could have been a prolonged dream in my semi-coma-induced state. I didn't quite know which part was true…

Levian's feelings for me were obviously real which meant the ardour or psychic parts were all ultimately true. Olive and I definitely did fall out because there were no expression of surprise on her face when I called Levian and Grayson to stay back in the room with me and not her. It may have not been a fight where I blamed her for my aunt dying but it was definitely a reason which made me treat her with passivity.

The Hallows could *actually* be my real parents all along but even in my ruptured, hanging-by -the-cliff imagination, I knew some part of my resentment and consternation within their sight had to be true somehow. My pulse quickened as Grenitch walked towards my hospital bed, I didn't know how long I was here for but it seemed like visiting hours should be over now even if it was a private hospital. "How are you feeling?", he asked in his low barbaric voice that didn't miss its snarl when he curved his mouth upwards. I guessed it was an attempt at a smile, one that I wish didn't startle the life out of me.

"I'm okay", I said trying to remember that I was still alive and needed to time every breath I took. Mrs. Hallows left the room to talk to the nurse and I was left with Gregnitch.

Even if she was just a figurine, I needed my Aunt Brie at this moment… more than anything and my frenzy must have called out the most psychotic part in me because I could have sworn, I could hear her voice play out in my head. "Don't react Esme darling, believe in what you can do and he won't be able to hurt you". I took a deep breath as Gregnitch walked closer to my hospital bed. "You remember what happened in the accident right? I'm surprised you even made it out alive", he said searching me for a sign that would explain how I did make it alive. A suspicion that crossed my head still wanted me to believe this was all just a pretence and the federation did actually exist. "You're the reason I'm here, aren't you?", I asked suddenly, a lightbulb flashing in my head.

"You're mistaken, you hurt your consciousness in that accident so you'll jump to conclusions as you did with that boy outside", he said but his ruthless tone told me everything I needed to know. "You hurt me again", I said softly. "I may have thought of you doing a lot worse in my head but one thing I do recognize for sure is that YOU hit me several times and I'll be damned if that wasn't what happened at the lake during my 'accident'". His silence told me everything. "You're my legal father? My birth father?", I continued in mock astonishment. "I still remember everything *Gregnitch.* You've been hurting me forever but this is too far now and I'm standing up for it."

"Sounds a bit cocky for the girl stuck in her bed, you're crazy", he replied standing up, squaring his shoulders. I noticed his eyes grow larger in anger and spotted a shadow of Levian and a hospital member standing outside the slightly ajar door. "I'm not crazy enough to think you've been physically abusing me for all my life, defiling my presence. My state is because of you and you should be rotting in jail right now", I said, my aversion unmuffled and distinct. My last statement seemed to have made him lose his temper as in an instant I had the grown man on top of me, his hand reaching for my throat as I lifted my burnt, contused hands to push him off me but in vain. He was much too strong… I was a seventeen-year-old girl, sitting in a hospital bed because of being mutilated by this man, recovering from an accident while being maimed once more. There are always dark and light times in life that I had observed in what I could arrange in bits and pieces from my whole life whether any of those memory serums were real or not and while my mental state was far beyond normal, I could distinguish between pure and evil.

Right now, at this moment, I saw a wave of darkness wash over me that I had never before. It filled me with self-loathing and abhorrence. For being in this situation, for having to endure it for so long, for not being able to ever totally free myself from this very thing. It was a scenario I can never quite bring myself to describe the entire version of events because of how devasting it is. I could never see the world the same way again despite how many times I had to encounter the same situation repeatedly but it wasn't just a beating of belts. It was death's nemesis that seemed to have been gifted to me and I would have chosen to be gasping for breath in a gas chamber instead of that sinful hospital bed.

My throat was pressed down against his murderous fingers, as he pinned my hands down and tied them together with the handcuffs swiftly to keep me from struggling against his attack. My eyes kept blurring out and I expected to pass out anytime soon but that would have been a blessing. He struck me with several blows. A punch above my abdomen before he whipped a belt out from nowhere and whipped my stomach with it. Each hit, was harder than the previous one. "Slash, Bham!", came the sounds of the belt as I refrained from screaming to hold my dignity, my defiance of my honour shining through the pain although it was also because my throat was being constricted from making any noise and I was certain my vocal cords were broken. My entire body jolted up and down as the belt came down even faster.

Gregnitch swore the whole time as he brought down every whip of his belt. I could feel the respite of the warm blood starting to trickle down my stomach but my foolish hope of him stopping there was long since discarded.

He brought down more whips on the cuts, my body burning like it was on fire, on spikes while being dipped in poison concurrently. I used my entire will to use my feet to kick at him in his moment of weakness as he paused for breath as I aimed for his face, trying to crawl out of the bed with whatever little movement I could make as his grip over my throat slipped for a moment. I couldn't swallow at all, and my throat couldn't physically take gulps of air or make any sound so I tried to keep breathing and focus on my saliva intake. I made quiet whines as I made for the door on the other side of the room, attempting to run outside but Gregnitch was too quick for me.

He caught me, threw the belt aside, tempered and heated because of my kick as he in return lunged out for me using his feet which I narrowly missed and continued running towards the door, my hands still handcuffed. Tears streamed down my eyes in hopelessness as Gregnitch lunged out for the door, locked it and pushed me down with unaccountable force. My adrenaline was rushed against my weakness from my injury which caused me to fall limp as Gregnitch dragged me across the floor by my hair and pinned me to a hook in the wall by my clothes before he took out the belt again and started whipping me… This time it wasn't my stomach, it was much higher and much lower…The place in my body that should be universally revered the most like every other sign of womanhood. I begged my throat to scream as I felt my body go through tarnished heaps of pain. They say a woman's body is her temple but at that moment, it had become a blasphemous rock of shame that was enduring a beating it shouldn't. Whipping it should never have seen. It was way beyond repulsive.

I wanted to faint to stop seeing it, my debilitated body had lost its last will to fight as running across the room had taken everything out of me and I had no voice left. The tears were the only thing alive in me except for my presence of mind as my entire body was convulsed from the shock and gnawing of pain in every part. My mouth opened and closed as my teeth bared out to try to make it stop. To beg for mercy, to beg for help. But the fight in me had gone, this was my faith and it made me miss the worst time before this I had been hurt by the Hallows. My chest had been profoundly flattened, I was sure I had nothing but broken ribs and my stomach felt twisted and I was certain my intestines were going to pop out at any second as my legs were paralysed.

I was pulled off the hook then and even then, a little engraving of hope believed the deflation to cease but I was wrong once again. I was pushed faceward to the ground and kicked as I felt Gregnitch jump on me with his feet using his full force and a few more spatters of blood informed me that my teeth and nose were broken. He pulled me up by my head again as my legs and stomach remained rested on the ground, my head spinning as my head was brutally held up until a sharp edge cut through the edge of my cheek. The skin tore as the silver blunt of a knife appeared. With an unusual doubt of will, I forced myself to turn over although I couldn't feel anything in my body but the blood and pain that had just transformed into numbness.

I held up my handcuffed hands as a shield, covering my bleeding face as the knife's edge cut through the handcuffs, freeing my arms. I tried to use it to get up but stumbled to my back instead as I caught sight of Gregnitch's face. His eyes were full of repulsive hatred. His mouth still stretched apart from the enormity of the nefarious words he addressed me with as he ruined my physical being, my body, my temple… Girls complain about their insecurities with their bodies all the time and at this moment, when I was trying desperately to save what was left of it, I felt a deep sense of distaste for such girls. Olive was one of them, she had the healthiest figure yet hated the way her body looked, thinking she had too many curves, too many flaws. What she never could realise was how lucky she was to have each unharmed curve. To go home every day with those curves still intact, to know that the precious bits of her body would only be cared for by her or whoever she provided consent to…

I had lost that right and I couldn't even create any sound about it because that privilege had been mangled right before my eyes. It was cruel to leave nothing but my eyes so I could feel the pain, see the bruises and the scars, and see my young self-get ruined at the hands of a man who claimed to be my biological father. The man who helped create me also helped ruin me. Slowly and erroneously, tormenting every bit of life in me until there was nothing left to attack. Nothing left to demolish. Nothing left of me to doom. Gregnitch's face was unflinching, his nostrils flared, and his fingers wrapped tightly around the knife that was finally going to end my suffering. End the darkness and the bleeding and rescue that sacrilegious mess he had made my body or leave it here in that hospital room as my life corroded with it. I longed for death to rescue me at that moment as I was prepared for that knife to end the purgatory I was faced with. I didn't bother to squeeze my eyes shut as I spread my hands out in surrender, welcoming the relief of death the knife was going to bring me with its final stab and a final gush of blood. It came nearer and nearer as all I could see was the knife's silver point, my last thought in this world.

A large sound distracted its contact with my face as heavy thuds filled the air. My eyes scrolled upwards as I felt myself being lifted off the ground as screams filled around me that I couldn't pay attention to. I felt the warm, familiar hands of Levian lift me up as I sank against his chest trying to get my eyes to close to block out the pain and the agony I felt in that situation. From the parts I could see of Levian and my exsanguinated hospital gown, my blood was covering him as the blurry looks of hospital security filled the place. I felt myself get placed onto another platform I couldn't make out because my eyes were drooping from the pain. This must be the time of my slow death, in this very hospital. The sound of the police, and frantic screams of voices sounded familiar to me but I didn't care… My eyes were half opened the entire time and I clung to Levian with whatever strength I had remaining which was probably in the negatives by now. His harm didn't leave my side for a second as the world spun around me and my entire face wobbled as I threw up all over my condemned, defiled chest and a bit on the part I could see of Levian's. More pain soared up my body as my knotted stomach threw up all its contents.

Life works a funny way when we associate memories with other times. The last time I ever threw up was back at Brie's when I was filled with custard tarts that Brie and I had agreed to try out for a change from the cakes and lemon tarts we always had from tea which resulted in both of us throwing up all over the carpet as we helped each other clean up and hold each other's hair. We laughed for days after that, vowing to never try out Cassy's new deserts ever again despite that woman supplying the most fabulous cakes and tarts. Or the other time when I puked out my entire glass of beer after having too much at Patrick's birthday where things fell to disaster. When I fell out with Olive after the Grayson situation. It didn't seem so awful to me at present. much more of a distant, nostalgic memory. If they even existed. If this wasn't my reality and my apparent 'dreams or schizophrenic recollections were actually true. Nothing felt light at that moment as darkness swelled around me, rotting on its doubled layers of pitch black with my aching body. More tears shot out of my eyes like bullets. It was a wonder I could produce so much water now when I couldn't even use them to defend myself anymore. Aunt Brie was wrong. He did hurt me and she wasn't here to protect me this time because she never was there, my power was *non-existent,* it was *hopeless,* it was never *real.* The light that water always gave me was gone, it breached me and destroyed me. I had lost the light I needed the most to save me. More tears…

CHAPTER 22

Levian or Grayson

Levian hadn't left my side even when the nurses rushed to put me in the ER. I was fed painkillers and dozed off because as soon as I opened my eyes, I saw Levian asleep on a chair, his neck twisted as it fell on the back of the chair. He looked extremely uncomfortable but the thought of him just being there made me happier and also made me wonder if Grayson would have done the same. Where was Grayson anyway at this time?

If he was telling the truth, I might have just flipped off my chances with Grayson but if he wasn't then I had moved on from another failed, noxious romantic relationship. Was I willing to risk it with my best friend? I had no idea but I always had a kindling that Levian felt much more for me than just a best friend and maybe I reciprocated some amount of that feeling but at the same time I couldn't be disallowing the fact that I could have just appreciated the comfort I got from that adoration.

A nurse entered the room with Olive telling her she could stay for fifteen minutes as she cautiously tiptoed towards my bed. "Hey", she whispered sitting at the edge. She glanced over at Levian and gave me a knowing smile. "What?", I asked sheepishly and tried not to make it obvious that I knew what she was hinting at. Levian. "You look like you fought a war love", Olive said disquieted and I knew the reason behind her not immediately reaching out to extend her comfort through physical tough was because my injuries were probably worse than I believed. I hadn't seen them yet but a little part of me told me to expect the best.

"I've been fighting since I was 11", I replied glancing at Levian to see if we woke him. He must be a pretty sound sleeper as he tried to turn over on his chair, grunting in his sleep. I didn't know if Olive really knew what all I meant with my mind distorted as it was but I did know that she knew I went to boarding school and I did suffer from domestic abuse for a while even if it was fighting off the federation.

I sighed. If only I had stayed in Abilo and never gone to that lake again. I should have never followed that horse. Suddenly a lightbulb in my head clicked. "Levian wake up!", I shouted without thinking as he sat up instantly, with an expression that made him look prepared to fight someone off. He may have been pretty shaken by what happened to me too, he must really care about me. "Liah, what happened?", he asked, a little annoyed. "Levian, do you remember AMBROSIA?? I had a horse called Ambrosia, right?". Ambrosia was my refuge in Kipsy City so maybe she was still there. He nodded matter of facedly "Yeah she lives with that aunt of yours, the one who's a horse breeder, are you seriously planning on going there right now?", he asked. "Esme, you've been badly injured just an hour ago, you're not going anywhere", Olive said sternly causing me to stick my tongue out at her childishly. "Olive, I'll forgive you for what happened at Patrick's party, if you find a way to get me there.", I said in rebellion. It was downright wicked of me to turn her own guilt against her but I was desperate.

I noticed Olive and Levian exchange glances as the doors suddenly opened again. The nurse was back with Grayson as she scooted Olive out of the room letting Grayson take his turn for visiting hours. He locked eyes with me and didn't move any closer to my bed like Olive did when she entered and instead chose to say, "Esme, they took Mr. and Mrs. Hallows to the police station, I think you're not gonna be able to live with them for a while because your mother needs to be at the hearing for your father for attacking a minor patient and all the other charges the hospital pressed against him". Typical Grayson, candid more than comforting.

Levian got up from his chair and shot a dirty look at him. "Grayson, you have no reason to be here when she told you to leave before". Grayson just shrugged not taking his eyes off mine. "It's fine", I said. After the attack, I didn't want to be alone and again and I selfishly didn't want Grayson to stay away from me in either reality. The one he made everyone think I was fabricating or this hospital one that I couldn't seem to leave.

"I want to go to my aunt's to see Ambrosia", I said, actively speaking to both of them waiting for a brainwave to somehow get me there. "I'll take you", Grayson said almost at once as Levian snorted in protest. "Are you crazy? The hospital isn't going to let her leave at all". I rolled my eyes, I loved Levian but sometimes I doubted if his love for me was growing into an obsession or if he was just really precautious. "Lev, she can't stay in here forever and she wants to", Grayson replied. For the first time, I badly wanted Grayson to win this fight as I rested my head back against my pillow.

"I don't care, someone just please take me out, I have enough medication to heal", I said trying not to sound as exasperated as I felt. My whole life just felt like one giant ball of chaos and I couldn't seem to leave it. "Okay fine, let's make you a deal then", Grayson said walking closer to my bed, Levian's fingers twitched nervously.

"One week of rest and we'll take you in Lev's car, okay? Just the three of us and nobody else", Grayson said diplomatically and I had to agree. It was better than nothing. "What about Olive?", Levian piped in and I inwardly groaned. I didn't sign up for this to be a friend's day out when I just wanted to see my horse and this aunt I hadn't ever heard of because it was evident, I had to be living with some kind of relative when I got out of the hospital because I was not going to be roommates with Mrs. Hallows for sure.

"Olive has to go home anyway, her parents won't allow her to traipse around when it's after hours to god knows where", Grayson said confidently. I didn't know what he meant by it being after hours but I was going to leave it at that. The nurse called Grayson out after his visiting hours were over and I was left with Levian. "Well, I'm looking forward to this week getting over so I can finally get out of this hospital bed and see my horse. Oh, and maybe study so I *actually* get into college and become a marine biologist while I'm at it", I said chirpily. He repositioned himself so he was sitting right next to me, leaning his head over mine. "I know she missed you, Ambrosia", he said planting a kiss on the top of my head. "I'm really sorry about what happened Liah, you shouldn't have had to deal with it".

"You have nothing to be sorry for Levian, thank you for always being there for me", I replied. I couldn't turn around to look directly in his face on account of being heavily dozed and bandaged. "You didn't break any bones you know? You're just always so strong", he remarked. I laughed, in the most senile mine, one could know I wasn't strong. I was nothing without my powers and nothing without knowing what was happening to me. That's the problem with being a victim of something tragic when people always assume that because you've undergone serious a set of serious misfortunes, you're automatically a person who's stable when it could not be falser for me.

I recognized myself being a victim of several tragedies, some of that I ignited myself yet I had the most unstable mind despite having to be a fighter all the time. "Not every soldier has strength Levian and I'm not even in the army", I commented with a delirious 'heh'.

"Well, they should have you someday but I would not want to lose you", he said. It was wonderful how I could feel his breath over my head yet he somehow managed not to add any pain to my pulsating limbs. "You know what I see in my dreams Esme? Or my 'rotating liah' as I refer to them even if I get lesser than you do?". I shook my head. "I see the day you came over with your tiny legs because you were just a child back then, like me and giving me food since your house was so close to mine and enveloping me in the warmest hug when my parents died and I was grief-stricken beyond words. You helped me heal back then and I can't ever return that favour". I couldn't believe he had actually revealed that piece of information about himself. "Wait Levian, you can return that favour", I said in a determined voice. I had to know for real if there was any chance the federation did actually exist before I could make up my mind to trust Grayson again. "On that ride to my aunt's stables, we're going to first go to your house".

CHAPTER 23

Larson's Stables & Farm

Grayson had kept to his promise as exactly one week from our deal, the doctor gave me the green flag to be allowed outside for a stroll after regulating my pulse and making sure I didn't suddenly burst into anymore nightmares or wake up in the middle of the night screaming. It was true I had the most juvenile nightmares every day but that was only expected and I would wipe off the sweat from my neck and arms so it didn't interfere with my plan.

Levian visited me at the hospital every day of the week, bringing me things to occupy my time. I would read or make bracelets when I was bored as he brought tiny little wooden handicrafts, he made himself like miniature wooden dolls and boats. Mrs. Hallows as the nurse mentioned had called in to check in on me but was busy in court ensuring her husband's case was made and didn't ruin him completely but I didn't want to waste a single thought on that.

I managed to walk every now and then without help and the wincing gradually decreased every time I stepped out of bed. I was still bandaged and given stitches on my face and stomach but my intake of painkillers had stopped which was a good sign although I wouldn't have minded them continuing my supply for a few more days as I still woke up every morning feeling awfully sore. effulgence

"You ready to go, Lev got his car out", Grayson said swinging his bag over his shoulders as he entered the hospital room with Levian. He hadn't visited me even once after our deal so a part of me felt like he was just being gracious. "Yeah, I just need to sign a few papers first and then I'm allowed to but we'll have to be back before 8", I replied signing on the sheets the nurse provided me. I was all ready today. Olive had dropped off some spare clothes of hers so I was decked out in a comfy pair of blue cargo pants, a tight-fitted, yellow t-shirt that had sunflowers embroidered across it and brown boots. I wouldn't necessarily pick the dazzle of this outfit to be one of effulgence but they were comfortable enough for me to be able to hold myself in. Olive was also a few sizes larger than me so her clothes just hung loose over my body, not hugging the curves it should. Hospital food would make anybody lose too much weight to not have clothes hug you the way they should.

Levian took his car out after he helped me into the front and Grayson slid into the back whipping out his mobile. "It's 40 minutes away", he announced setting an online location directory on as the voiceover gave Levian the details. "After this, we go to your house?", I asked Levian, leaning towards him to make sure Grayson couldn't hear. Grayson would know all about the Rotating Liah even if he hadn't seen it and would stop me if he knew my plan. Levian inclined his head in my direction and turned up the radio as Hello World by the Tremeloes played at the full groove. "What is this rubbish?", Grayson demanded from the backseat and Levian and I laughed as we sang loudly along to the song. Levian and I would be the only two people at our whole school who would love bands like the Tremeloes and the Avett Brothers because of how matched their songs were with our moods, our life themes and just the overall lyrical structure that we felt creep up to our bones. It was the best feeling in the world.

When I woke up one early morning feel blue oh so blue
I opened back the curtains and the sun shone through
Hello World, today I feel like someone
Hello World, today I sing a bad song

A glint of a tear shone in my eyes. Aunt Brie loved the Tremeloes as much as I did. I would read my book out on the couch staring at the tiles as she would dance unnoticedly to their songs or quote them to me randomly. "Yeah, it's right, you are singing a bad song", Grayson whined, continuing to complain. "Shut up Grayson. She likes it and she's the patient who also happens to be sitting in the front seat", Levian said. I giggled, Levian was way beyond obsessed with the Tremeloes and if this was his way of making Grayson shut up, I was okay with it. We didn't bother having many conversations on the journey due to Levian paying attention to both the directions and the song and I was perfectly fine being silent all ride while Grayson chattered away about how Zara and Marshall were going out together for dinner and how he blew off Patrick to hang out with us today. He continued about his new record time during swim practice which perplexed me because I never knew he learnt swimming in the first place but I let him talk.

We approached the gates of my aunt's stables as the gatekeeper let us in. I stuck my head out of the window, taking a gulp of fresh air like a dog. The air felt so pure around here, you could almost drink it. The skies were blue and filled with pinkish, greyish clouds as the sun radiantly showed its light on the green, luscious lawns and trees that were well-manicured. These weren't some ordinary stables or farms, they were lawns of it as horses and cows lazily hung around the lawns, kicking at their feet and neighing in pleasure at the day's pulchritude.

"It's beautiful", Levian exclaimed as we got down and walked toward the stables where the gatekeeper told us we'd find my aunt. "You nervous? You haven't seen her in a while but she's expecting you, your mother passed the news, she knows you're coming here", Levian said as I glanced around the horses kept behind their stable doors, some stable keepers feeding them with hay and apples. "Mrs. Hallows?", I asked bemused. "Yeah, she knew she'd be at court so she called your aunt ahead of time". Grayson walked up to a woman petting a black stallion, dressed in riding gear. "Hi, do you know where the owner of these stables is? A Miss Hallows I'm assuming?". She turned around to face Grayson, her eyebrows creased in confusion. "Ahh yes I do, are you the child I'm expecting dear?". I gulped, my mouth being very aware of its saliva suddenly. Her face was unmistakable. There was no way…

"No, it's actually my friend Esme here", Grayson answered pulling me in front of him for my aunt to get a clear view of me. "Well, I happen to be the owner so you're in luck and my goodness Esme, aren't you a rather nubile young lady now? Which one of these boys is your chosen suitor? She laughed jokingly, wrapping me in a gigantic hug. "Welcome to the Larson's Stables, stay as long as you like", she said giving me a wide smile as I returned a rather forced one of my own. There was no doubt about it. This woman was definitely Aunt Brie. She both talked and looked like her so whatever game Mrs. Hallows was now playing was thoroughly flummoxing…

CHAPTER 24

The Cycle

Aunt Larson was the visual representation of Aunt Brie, she even talked like her but she didn't seem to remember a thing obviously. I would never understand why Mrs. Hallows ever showed me any mercy by finally allowing me to be by my aunt but my best guess was that the cycle continued that way. A confrontation of my water powers to go back to Brie's and every time there is a memory serum involved. My name held a newer meaning in itself. Esmerliah wasn't about a water creature at all. It was a water cycle. It surfaced a cycle of self-esteem I managed to keep throughout every time the cycle flows and ripples. It was like the sea, past present or future, I would end up in the same fight all over again until the Hallows got what they wanted and now again I was back to the same thing. Small bits of happiness with my Aunt Larson who I could very well figure out was Aunt Brie considering Levian's figurine was Brie Larson who played Captain Marvel. She was the same person regardless.

Larson had invited us over for some peanut butter sandwiches and handed apples all around as she indulged in polite conversation while asking me how I was doing since my accident. She treated me warmly yet her demeanour was still that of a stranger's and it rubbed my feathers the wrong way. Levian and Grayson seemed to like her as much as they did Aunt Brie back in Snakes and Ladders so they were definitely warming up to the idea of me living out in the stables. "So, you are planning on staying here in Detroit right Esmerliah?", she said addressing me. I flinched at the use of my whole name, it gave it way too much power, too much of an expectation to continue the cycle.

"Well, I will be fully released from the hospital in a couple of days I think so I will be returning to boarding school if I'm still enrolled", I replied sharply. "Oh honey, you can stay here you know, your mother already made arrangements until your family crisis is settled", Larson said getting up to take the reins of a new horse being walked into the stables by a rider. That was who I was, a new horse every time the ocean called for a low tide after a high tide. Every time I was turned into something fragile after fighting confrontation. Returning to aunt *Larson* as she always took me by the reins to guide me. "So, I'm going to be living with you then?", I asked pointedly and Grayson shot me a dirty look. He seemed more intent on getting me settled than I was but a good guess of mine said it came from guilt.

Larson didn't seem to take my ungrateful remark to heart and continued her pleasant tone. "Only if you wish to darling, I always loved you like my own and well I know I'm the only family you have left so I do hope you choose to. You can finish your last year of school too". I replied with a half-hearted smile. I didn't know why I was being so cynical about this arrangement. Aunt Brie lapsed into the conversation about turning her little cottage into an extension of some old stables for a suite room for me while Grayson reciprocated her enthusiasm claiming he would love to visit all the time.

Levian silently got up and I followed him as he walked over to the horse the trainer had brought, relieving Larson of her duties. “I think Esme would love to be reunited with Ambrosia, wouldn’t she?”, he said finally adding his own say to the conversation as Grayson started asking Levian for his opinion on having a haystack put in my converted suite as a ‘hangout couch’. I went over to the horse and petted her mane as she neighed against my touch. A golden crown settled on her head and caught my attention as I looked back and forth between her and Larson. It was the tiara I had made for her the night I was at the lake; Ambrosia had been with Brie the last time which confirmed my last suspicion. Grayson had won the game and stuck up a deal with the Hallows but there was nothing I *could* do about it. If Mrs. Hallows had sent me to Larson, she was only continuing the same cycle… the thought kept revisiting my head. It was always going to be under the Hallows’s rule. The federation was never the real enemy, they only enforced rules by the Hallows because *they* were the real nemesis who toyed with me. Repeatedly, because they created me in that lab. I was their experiment in that lab and they believed they owned me. Brie never rescued me; she was always part of their cycle and that was their plan all along. To see how many different realities, I could endure with different reactions. It was a sick mind game they played like I was their doll. I didn’t even need to go to the Rotating Liah anymore to remind Levian of his memories, it was no use.

“What are you thinking of?”, Levian asked me as he stroked Ambrosia’s mane. “It sounds perfect after everything that has gone down”. He helped me get on the horse’s back as the trainer brought out another horse for Levian to ride. I grinned at the sight of Grayson and Aunt Larson continuing to share their excitement for my new bedroom suite, it felt nice to see Grayson make so much effort to get to know my family member still and I think I understood in an incredibly twisted way. "Exactly it's extremely perfect", I said not taking my eyes off them. "So why the hesitation?", Levian pressed as we walked our horses out onto the manicured lawns. The sky was still clear, with its clouds fluffed up and dense, their pinkish hue beginning to compliment the clear blueness of the sky's expression.

"I think there's been enough of a cycle dealing with attaining the perfect", I said, my words giving me a whole new sense of purpose. "I'm breaking it today right here in this place because I despise the control and I will never be able to be happy if I chase after the perfect future, the perfect, present and the perfect past when truly I know they'll always remain imperfect just like our friend group". We increased our speed to a trot as Levian replied with heaves, "You don't want to live with her then? Where will you go?". He looked like he digressed deciding not to question me further. He knew I was referring to the Hallows and Grayson in some way. "I was thinking about living with you for a little while before I figure out how to change it completely", I said tentatively biting my upper lip. I hoped this wouldn't get awkward especially when I was fully aware of Levian's feelings towards me.

"I can never say no Esme and while I may not fully understand I know you have some wicked plan of yours that makes it sensible. However, I do think it's not a good idea for you if you're still in love with *him*". Levian almost spat those words out and I could tell he was referring to Grayson.

I grinned as I brought our horses to a halt as we circled back to the stables where Grayson was still engrossed in a gratifying conversation with Larson.

I quickly jumped off and pulled Levian down as well until Grayson had a clear sight of us over my aunt's shoulder. I clasped my hands behind Levian's neck and pressed my mouth to his firmly as his fingers slid around my waist, hugging me in a firm grip. Time seemed to fall slow. It was like in those movies where everything appeared in slow motion. My peripheral view passed me the satisfaction of seeing Grayson's fist clench by his sides as he got up hastily, evidently blithering in what I at least hoped was resentment or a sudden need to go to the bathroom. Don't get me wrong, I didn't kiss my best friend to make the guy I was in love with jealous after he had wronged me. Teenage love is confusing, it's weird, and it's almost unearthly. But it's imperfect at the same time when teenager hormones go wild as they struggle through their life problems in such a century where the whole world seems to rest on their shoulders. Sometimes things work and other times they don't but it is important to break whatever cycle you are accustomed to if you want to move on. Kissing Levian wasn't the same as kissing Grayson but if I chose to continue kissing Grayson, he would be pulling me back in the cycle as he was always part of it. Levian was unplanned and therefore helpful to break that chain. With him, our affection ran slow while time seemed to break its scientific details and run like there was a break in between worlds. A break for me to document every moment in my life. With Grayson, it was rushed, and it was frantic, it was as if time would not wait for us so we had to rush our heads into a paroxysm of frenzy to enjoy each other.

They were both beautiful and at this moment as I pulled away from Levian, I knew I had chosen right. Grayson was a fantasy but he was also reality while Levian was always reality but turning into the fantasy I had never had. One with peace and not chaos because there was enough magic and light in my life, the type I had never asked for. I rested my forehead against Levian's as he gave the sweetest smile ever and hugged me tightly. "Thank you, Esme,", he said without any explanation but I accepted his gratitude. I had a lot to thank him for as well. "Aunt Larson", I said walking over to her. She was too busy instructing her trainer with some of her horses to notice her niece's public display of affection. "Yes darling, are you ready to move in? I can sign over the necessary paperwork at the hospital". She said smilingly. "I returned her smile saying, "Thank you so much for your hospitality but I think I have different plans for now but I will come to visit you every weekend for sure. I can't say goodbye to either you or Ambrosia forever". "I totally understand and of course, you're a responsible young woman Esmerliah, good luck!".

I nodded as we started walking back out. "Oh, and one more thing", I said abruptly. "Thank you for letting me forget and for believing". My words left her nonplussed as she replied saying, "Of course honey, no problem!" and we got back into Levian's car. "I'm assuming you plan on living in the hospital forever then", Grayson muttered. I shook my head as Levian answered for me. "She's living with me, *Gray*". I forced back a laugh at the mockery. "Oh, I have an idea Levian, if we're moving in together. I think it's been a while since we've partied and I want to toast to new beginnings with cheap beer as I figure out the rest of my schoolwork too so what do you say we throw a housewarming when I move in with you?", I ask. Grayson perked up at this, he loved parties. "Oh yes that's a good one Esme, can I bring my guitar?", he asked chirpily and Levian granted him permission. "Alright we'll let the others know", he said and I squeezed his hand. Grayson's eyes flitted to the action and I tried not to notice him staring hard at me. I knew he was marvelling at the sudden change and choice I made but it was the way to go. Breaking another thing in the cycle seemed salient even if it was the most flowery part. Patrick's parties. Nothing ever was fully successful at his parties or celebration which meant that had to be broken and moving it to Levian's seemed only right. A new beginning also meant an end to the old cycle. An end to having to forget and fight.

CHAPTER 25

A Moment of Calm

Paperwork is always so incredibly boring… As soon as I was given the green flag to leave the hospital, I decided to go straight to Levian's house. I wasn't sure where all my stuff was and according to some messages Mrs. Hallows left me, the house was under police supervision and closed off while they investigated Gregnitch's other crimes that had illegal drug and technology plans. No doubt the genetic solutions and illegal creation of a designer baby were kicking him back now from his federation days despite having used the memory serum for everyone in the city. It's always hard when your own creation goes against you, isn't it? In this case, the memory serum samples found itself were illegal so I decided to go later to the house and claim my remaining items. In the meanwhile, Aunt Larson supplied me with things she thought would be useful and Olive helped out as well.

Levian already had all the necessary things one would need in a house which was remarkable for someone who lived by himself so all I did pack was one suitcase and one carry bag comprised of all the things I had been supplied with. When I reached Levian's house, he already had a chair decked out for me covered in blue and gold paint, my favourite colours and a plate of lemon tarts set out. It was the best welcoming gift ever. "Larson said she'll come over during our housewarming party and you can bring your doll too, the one you keep talking about", Levian said cheekily while unwrapping the paper on the Thai curry boxes he ordered for takeout. I punched him playfully saying, "Don't insult Betty, she's my best friend". I meant it. The last time I had seen her was in the game but I had no clue where she would be right now, without her magic. I wondered what she would even look like.

Several hours passed before we both decided to take a little nap considering we were both exhausted in general. Levian woke me up in time to get changed for our housewarming. I looked at the dress lying in my suitcase. It was one of those flowy, trailing dresses that rippled like water. This one was particularly magnificent, it had a strapless top joined to the skirt part of the dress with a tight bodice aligned with shiny pearls at the bottom that broke into ripples of silk fabric, the back part of the dress almost at toe length. A note was attached to the back of the dress so I flipped it over and read it. My heart did a somersault as I saw an attachment of a very old note. The note that I had in fact left Aunt Brie when I left Abilo to go to the lake. My eyes scrolled over to the recipient of the note and I quickly scanned the page.

My dearest Esme

There is no doubt that the minute my eyes landed on your face despite the scars from your 'accident', I recognized exactly who you were and not just as some distant niece I am supposed to believe. I don't know what exactly happened to me but that night you left the stables I had a dream. One where you were around 11 with similar scars on your face and there was yelling as if someone was about to attack you. You were showing me how you could make your fingers light up with neat tricks once your fingers encountered the water and the later part of it was rather intense as well. I couldn't sleep after that dream because it felt so real somehow. So, I thought and thought and thought Esme, I racked my brains really hard because everything suddenly felt wrong. I went back to the stables to check in on Ambrosia suddenly and she was gone but there was the faintest trace of that light I saw in my dream. I walked into it, I breathed it and felt the light and then something just clicked in my brain. I remembered everything Esme, I don't even know if it's all real but I did. Which gives me the idea that you remember too because I could tell from your facial expressions when you met me as I analysed it after this brainwave I got. if you want to call it that. I don't even know how I'm still alive after the game Esme. Maybe I never actually died? Anyway, I thought about Betty Harbour who had come to visit me with a message from you right before the federation officials showed up. She was such a sweet girl Esme, misunderstood but sweet and we got the chance of getting to actually know each other better so sitting right there in those stables just suddenly reminded me of her. It wasn't your light Esme; I remember yours very clearly but it was hers. Like she had broken in and taken Ambrosia away. Betty was another Indifferent who had water powers and if you remember everything, I'm certain she does too and she might be trying to get involved with the Hallows or something searching for answers and I know each of the Indifferents would start to remember at some point so I'm going to go in search for her and try to help her in this weird new reality. Anyway, I have rambled on enough but here's a dress I thought you'd really like, I found it tucked away in my closet (It's an old dress of mine) and I thought you might take a fancy to it. I'm sorry I won't be able to stop by your friend's house today but I'm leaving in search of Betty so I might be unavailable for a while. My numbers on the next page if you need to reach out to me...

Love you always

Brie

PS: If you're trying too hard for your powers now, remember you'll be able to control them when you're at your calmest. Memory serums can't remove what's growing in you, Esme.

I flipped the page over to see her digits as a tear dropped on the page. I didn't even know why I was crying at this point. That letter had left me in a whirlwind of emotions and I didn't know how to tackle them at best. She remembered, and she was looking for Betty! Betty must have not lost her powers at all; she must have been lurking somewhere and decided to take Ambrosia after tracking Brie down. I had to find her but that meant I needed to be able to open a water portal in order to communicate with her. I didn't how she would reverse the damage the Hallows had done or stop them from hurting people altogether and I didn't even know what Betty's state was right now but today I needed to be able to harness my powers once more. I had to be calm.

I shoved the note into my suitcase and quickly pulled the dress over my head before shaking my hair loose down my shoulders. I stared back into my blue eyes in the reflection and then zipped my suitcase up and ran out as I heard the bell ring.

"Woah you look amazing", Levian exclaimed as he opened the door to let Grayson and Patrick inside. Grayson *had* brought his guitar and Patrick looked the exact same as I had seen him last. He dabbed Levian up and gave me a giant bear hug before he rushed into Levian's kitchen and began opening a few bottles of beers and breezers that Levian had laid out.

"Thank you Levian, you look great too", I answered grinning at my late reply that had been stalled by Patrick's entrance. He really did look stunning. He was wearing a grey turtleneck with a blue suit jacket over it that covered his arm muscles and brought out the colour in his eyes. I couldn't resist pulling Levian's mouth to mine and pushing against his shoulder flirtatiously. Seeing Grayson's jaw clench may have been the most satisfactory thing as he glared at Levian and set his guitar down with an extra thud. "Why are you so aggressive today?", Patrick asked him passing us each a bottle of beer that I readily refused seeing my plan was to calm down sober so the alcohol didn't infiltrate with my water magic senses.

Grayson smiled at him tranquilly. "Lev and Esme got together; I'm announcing my happiness for them". "They what??", Zara burst into the door with Marshall and Olive as everyone began greeting each other. "Finally,", Olive said with a forced smile, something told me she wasn't entirely happy with this. "So, when did this happen?", Zara asked excitedly jumping up and down. "When I kissed her and she chose Levian", Grayson said with brutal honesty as Zara's face fell. I think Grayson got the same satisfaction from Zara that I got from him. "Y'all kissed?", she asked hesitantly. "Don't worry Zara, it was just one kiss wasn't it Grayson? I mean I can't even *remember* much of anything", I said as I fluttered my eyelashes at him. He knew what I meant, he was another Indifferent who remembered so it was about time Olive and Levian did too. I had gone to the usual place where the Rotating Liah was placed in Levian's house but it wasn't there anymore. It was now just empty space that Levian claimed was there for us to dance on which is exactly what we all did.

I stopped trying to force my water powers to magically appear and instead just enjoyed myself throughout the party, treating myself to large gulps of coke that Levian had also set out with the breezers and beer and danced to the music all day. I slow danced with Levian when the Avett Brothers' song I loved came on, "I And Love and You" and I watched Zara and Grayson slide his arms around Zara and slow dance with her as well facing us. The pang of jealousy I would usually feel was replaced with a different feeling. I knew Grayson may have been trying to tug at my skin all evening but it wasn't working. I should be hysterical because a little part of me would always love Grayson no matter what. It's hard to forget your first real love, Levian *also* recognised that being my best friend but being with Levian may have been the rightest thing I had ever done. I stared at Grayson and Zara happily dancing over Levian's shoulder as everyone waved around sloppily under the effect of the alcohol and felt a strange wave of quietude slip over me. I felt at peace.

I felt happy. I looked into Levian's eyes and couldn't stop smiling. He smiled back. "You're beautiful Esme especially when you smile", he said and I rested my head back against his shoulder. This was undoubtedly one of the happiest moments in my life. "Y'all are so cute", Marshall said. He had taken Olive and Patrick's hands and begun to do an energetic dance routine with them and I was glad to see there was no hostility between them. It felt like everything was right again. I went to the sink to wash my hands as I had taken another bite of pizza and I felt a familiar surge of power soar up my fingers.

I looked down at them and twirled them around and golden specs of light burst out in the air. I laughed as a sense of duty called me and I excused myself telling Levian I had to use the bathroom. It was time to connect with Betty. I ran to the bathroom and heaved a huge sigh as I twirled my fingers with my eyes closed forming a golden portal. I was interrupted by Grayson who ran into the bathroom and locked the door behind him. "What are you doing?", he demanded angrily. He had no right to be angry. "Grayson, I'm doing what I have to do", I replied and continued working on the portal as he tried to stop it. It was too late; the magical golden light had formed something as Grayson in his attempts fell on top of me as I tripped underneath the sink as the golden portal flashed open…

CHAPTER 26

Water Portals

I gasped heavily under Grayson's weight as the magical wisps of golden light hovered in front of us almost daring me to enter. "You're not going in there Esme, you can't do that to Levian again", Grayson yelled anxiously as he got up and pinned my wrists against the sink. "It's only about time until he remembers. Until every one of the Indifferents remembers and wants a riot, you know BETTY won't just let the Hallows change everything again", I yelled back. I wasn't about to let Grayson ruin everything again for me. "Esme believe me, I've kept up with the news and I knew your aunt would remember as soon as we went there when I talked to her. I knew I shouldn't have saved everyone's lives.".

"SAVED?? Grayson, you TOOK their lives even if they aren't dead. After every memory serum, believe me, it's not fun knowing that you know absolutely nothing and I'm not going to go through that again. I'm not LETTING the Hallows own me". Grayson stood up and released his grip from my shoulders as I jumped up almost as quickly. With Mr. Hallows being in jail and Mrs. Hallows shipping me to live with Aunt Brie in this reality, it was all too obvious. "The Hallows will keep treating me as their prime experiment, the federation doesn't even matter nor will your life", I said. The bathroom door flung open for a second time and

Grayson and I both looked at each other in confusion as an unexpected visitor walked in. "I heard you'd be here", said the crisply mocking voice of Mrs. Hallows.

The music seemed to have stopped downstairs, I tried to stop the communication portal but it was still shining in golden light, attempting to contact Betty. "What are you doing here?", I asked irritated. This woman really managed to create the most morbid framework of thought. By sound, I could tell Levian and the others were rushing to the bathroom to see what Mrs. Hallows was doing.

"I'm your mother Esme, you'll treat me right", said she. I scoffed at her remark as I whisked my hand around until I concentrated golden light on the woman, I loathed most in the world and blasted her out of the bathroom. The pressure of the light may have been too much as the bathroom flooded with water everywhere as the taps, toiled at the shower filled up with water quickly.

Grayson fastidiously, pulled me out and screamed for everyone to get out of the house. I grabbed Grayson's hand as I used my light to break through a window and launched us out of the house on a swing as I noticed my golden blaster had pushed Mrs. Hallows outside as well. Convenient.

Marshall and Patrick had reached the bathroom at the same time, their knees now deep in water as they attempted to turn the taps off but they wouldn't budge and the water was rising up to stomach level now. "Get out, it's magic water", I screamed not knowing how to explain to my poor memory-wiped friends that they would not be able to control the water. Thankfully Levian pulled them out alongside a scared and frightened Olive and Zara and soon everyone was standing outside safely. I put my hands up again and tried to shield the water from leaving the house but it wasn't working. "That's not a portal Esme", Levian said frantically. "You created some sort of a weapon that fills up the place with the source of your powers". I was out of breath as I let go of my hands and sank to my knees panting. People were now crowding the streets as lots of blue and white officials holding guns also appeared on the scene, pushing my friends out of the way and trying to get the house under control.

"Lev, you remember?", Grayson asked tensely. It hadn't even occurred to me that Levian had suddenly managed to know about water portals, remembering the one I summoned to call Betty the last time and had also used my name instead of calling me 'Liah' like Betty did". "Of course, I remember Grayson, I remembered the second I laid my eyes on Esme after Mr. Hallows attacked her. I knew she'd want to live with me so we could work on her getting her powers back but she needed time and it gave me enough time to talk to her aunt and pass on the note and dress. I wasn't leaving her out of my sight in the meanwhile".

The water was unmanageable, my arms hurt from trying to contain it but more water kept flooding the street. It wasn't normal water, it had specs of golden light attached to its sides with increased speed. The water seemed determined to flood. "Well, this time you're getting locked up for good", Mrs. Hallows said as she played a morbid image of eleven-year-old me blasting the whole town of Kipsy with some kind of holographic gadget she had used to display the game rules. "We were finished with you in the game Esme, it's a shame Gregnitch couldn't finish beating you to death but now I think the general public will".

Of course, water had memory, the flood was making every person standing out on the road to remember every incident. It was an anti-memory effect I had managed to unlock. "Grayson you didn't do your job did you?", Mrs. Hallows said walking over to him as his jaw muscles twitched. "Keeping their memories lost was your one job in dealing with the power but now you watch your friend die instead of just knowing about it later. You *knew* not to let her get those powers back because it would reverse whatever effect we had. We can't afford Indifferents and now they all must die". Grayson looked sheepish as I shot him a look of disgust. The betrayal was thick.

The water was now at everyone's toes in the streets as I gave up trying to fix it knowing it wouldn't work and turned around to face the crowds of people walking towards me enraged as the water was evidently reminding them of the monster who destroyed their city once and time and time again. The water monster who destroyed Kipsy City. "You've gone too far girl", a towns folk called out. The federation officers walked towards me pinpointing guns at my head as I held my hands up in surrender. Tears rolled down my cheeks. I never meant for this to happen; I didn't know I was going to be the 'monster' again. Yet the water was gradually going to drown everyone and kill them and I wasn't strong enough to stop it.

The water was now ankle-deep and scores and scores of people were on the streets screaming and yelling for the flooding to stop. Screaming and yelling for the officers to shoot me since there was nothing, I could do to stop the water, Levian instantly stood in front of me, blocking the officer's range as another pointed a gun at his head too. "Kill them all, they're the monster's accomplices", townsfolk cried out as Grayson stood in front of Levian. Mrs. Hallows took that moment to step in front of a platform and use a microphone that she had got from nowhere saying, "This is the monster that's been tormenting the city, she's back like all the Indifferent's who want our city to be broken under their rebellious attempts to destroy us. She destroyed us once before and now she is doing it again. We can't make her forget so let's make her remember what happens to monsters. Who is with me? The leader of the Harbor Federation. The one who wants the good of our city since my husband has been trialled for this sleazy girl's attempt in pinning down defile as a charge against him. She must be killed and so must her accomplices".

A few people grabbed at parts of me but I was already ready to succumb, all my energy had disappeared into trying to control the water but it was failing. An angry man grabbed the nape of my neck and pushed me to sit down on my knees as an official aimed his gun at my head. People cheered and screamed in favour of Mrs. Hallows, evidently following the rule of the federation once again, forgetting that they would always be controlled. Several officials grabbed Levian and Grayson and pointed guns at their heads too. I wasn't having that; they were not at fault. Maybe Grayson a little, but he didn't deserve murder for not being able to follow Mrs. Hallow's rules perfectly. Levian certainly didn't and I would not let him die for me. I could not. I tried moving my hands to create another explosion or a cage to keep them safe but my wrists were tightly pinned behind my back by another official so I couldn't struggle as he shot me to death.

Cameras and phones were whipped out as people seemed to be recording the whole thing. No doubt for the press to congratulate the federation for taking care of Kipsy and Abilo city's water monster once and for all. Everything seemed hopeless. "ONE", the official called out as I shut my eyes tightly expecting death to shoot through my brain in two seconds. I was never going to defeat the game when the Hallows were the game, they owned it just as they owned me and now, they were stopping it. It was their world and I had just been a pawn in it. "TWO". I wondered what death would feel like. People usually experience their lives flash before their eyes but all I could ponder about was how it would feel like to have a bullet in my head. Would I be able to meet other dead people? Come think of it, I never experienced grieving for a dead person as after Brie's death, it was only a matter of seconds before it became a blood bath and everyone came back to the other reality the Hallow's created wiping everyone's memories. "THREE". This was it. A loud bang and I pushed my senses into feeling the force of the bullet in my brain, erasing all forms of life that I once consisted of. It was strange, maybe dying numbs you to feeling because as of now I couldn't really feel anything.

I cautiously opened my eyes and opened my eyes wide to see the officer in front of me lying on his back glassy-eyed just like the two other officers who had pointed guns at Grayson and Levian. They looked equally perplexed just like the townsfolk who looked just as slow in comprehending what had just happened. One look of agitation from Mrs. Hallows confirmed it all. "You're a shameful mother just like you are a shameful dictator", a scornful voice said loudly, grasping my attention.

Two figures floated on a cloud-shaped carpet with a watery outline of a bubble surrounding them. Betty and Brie. If they came from the house, it meant that I actually had created a portal. "You made Esmerliah Hallows, didn't you? That makes her your child and using her as a monster to make your position of control steady so people listen to you is pathetic. You're pathetic", Brie kept going. Her voice carried through the crowds as they listened aghast. Betty was holding a gun in her hands, one that I had no doubt she stole. She was in her full human figure this time as her silvery, cheeky voice reached out to me. "Ya portal worked Liah. Your magic just might take offence mode because of your incident with Gregnitch Hallows", she said as she casually fired her gun at the crowd shooting them. "You want a monster, well Betty Harbor is back for ya guys".

"Betty don't, they're innocent people", I said as Betty popped the bubble and she and Brie landed on their feet. "Get into the house girlie and take those friend things of yours too", she ordered and pushed me in with a good amount of force. The water seemed to have stopped flowing after her arrival and had been cleaned up almost as instantly. Some of the other federation officials were now rapidly shooting back at Betty and Brie as Betty renewed her bubble as **a** defence.

"You're a meddling, tiresome woman. Shoot her too", Mrs. Hallows screamed into the mic at Brie. I decided to obey

Betty instead of helping out and ushered Zara, Olive, Patrick and Marshal back into Levian's house as Levian and Grayson followed me inside. Everyone looked terrified and Levian ran to get glasses of water for everyone. A window shattered as an official aimed for the house and everyone jumped. "Thanks", I said to Levian, dipping my fingers into the water instead of drinking it and tried to feel the golden light again. I could still hear my aunt talking to Mrs. Hallows from outside.

"I went to a different town with Esmerliah to get away from you but you didn't seem too happy with that so you are the problem. ", Aunt Brie said. She seemed to be swaying the minds of some of the townsfolk as she explained a list of things the Hallows seemed to have done to terrorize both me and the towns.

"YA ARE THE PROBLEM HALLOWS", Betty yelled irked. "Maybe instead of all those memory serums you apply for people to forget about your mistakes, YA should forget about everything. YA can't keep people from seeing who you really are and how awful your dictatorship really is. It's morbid. "The crowd had turned on Mrs. Hallows now, all except the federation officers who now started indignantly shooting the innocent people who tried to get up to Mrs. Hallow's platform, considering Brie and Betty's impact.

Mrs. Hallows gave a deadpan glance at the two of them and yelled one word firmly and staidly. "SHOOT!". The federation officers immediately turned to them with their guns. There was no way Brie and Betty were going to be able to fend all of them off. Betty had shapeshifting powers and one gun; she wasn't enough. I raced as fast as I could through the front door with my glass of water despite everyone's protests and Grayson's feeble attempt of pulling me back again and threw the glass up into the air until I was completely drenched. I felt tingling sparks of golden light shine in my fingers. I had never felt such an abysmal mixture of emotions before. I was furious, determined to stop Mrs. Hallows for good and filled with both hope and fear that would end badly. I shot light into Betty's new gun and had it shoot back fast before the officials could press the triggers on their guns.

I was pushed backwards with a gigantic flash of light and the sound of a tuning fork being hit against my head as I shielded my eyes to see what happened. Light filled everywhere and everything. It was a solid three minutes before it stopped and I was being pulled to my feet by a grim-faced Betty. There was no other sound whatsoever.

CHAPTER 27

Goodbye Esme

"What happened?", I demanded as she pulled me into Levian's house where everyone was huddled in the kitchen. The flash of light had subsided as I followed Betty's glance outside the window. People lay spread-eagled all over the streets and I raised my hand to my mouth in chagrin. What had I done. Mrs. Hallows caught my sight, lying the same way almost as if she was dazed. Aunt Brie walked up to us and hugged me tightly as I folded my arms around her sobbing. "I am the monster from Kipsy City, I just killed them all", I cried as she soothed me.

"Liah, I have to tell ya something", Betty said quietly. "I stole the Rotating Liah from this house and Ambrosia after the game ended", she confessed. "Your boyfriend Levian told me all about it". I winced. I had a bad feeling about her confession as much as I wasn't used to hearing Levian being called my boyfriend. "The gun was a mini version, I shapeshifted it in the water and made it a bit more aggressive so ya not only took their memories away but ya also injured their brains to the point where they cannot remember very easily even with the right treatments. I mean it's possible but it would take a while, especially for Mrs. Hallows", she added. "How did you shapeshift the Rotating Liah Betty? You can only change your shape?", I asked annoyed at her voice for the first time around. "No, I can change the shapes of other things as well. There's more to it though Liah, the federation did not start in Kipsy City and the other officials from Abilo or other places will be tracing us down by this incident, we're not safe here". I sighed; I didn't know what else I could do.

I looked around at my friends who were looking at me a little dazed as they opened and closed their eyes. Levian and Grayson were attentively listening to the conversation differently, their faces hadn't changed. "Why are their faces doing that?", I asked pointing at the others. "They got hit a little by the blast so their memories are a little gone too and we must leave before they return", Betty explained. "Where will y'all go?", Levian asked attentively. Betty seemed to have it all sorted out.

"It's a place called Ludo", Brie explained. "It's where all the Indifferents are currently assembled, Betty and I rounded them off after I dropped off that letter to stop the federation from killing everyone once they realised everyone's memories had returned". "Like the board game? Shouldn't we be coming too?", Grayson asked inquisitively. "Eventually yes but we need two people to guard Kipsy while we make sure things are alright back there and yes like the ludo game, one of the Indifferent leaders created it after Snakes and Ladders to protect the Indifferents from the Federation. Away from the Hallows and it's the only place we'll be safe. Where Esme will be safe and where she can learn the roots of her powers", Aunt Brie explained. I nodded understanding perfectly well. After the blast, it was more than obvious, I wouldn't be safe here and neither would Betty or Brie or even Grayson and Levian. Levian turned his television on to see what the news was covering of the situation. It already flashed with details of the explosion and more officials coming to clean the place up and look for the Indifferents causing the trouble. News about Gregnitch escaping his trial also flared up on the screen. It was time to leave and go to Ludo.

"I think I should come too", I said after quickly grabbing the suitcase I left in my room. My dress had been torn on the sides after all the commotion and I didn't know if the Ludo headquarters had any clothes stocked. 'When do we go?", I asked. I was hoping to change first and say goodbye to everyone. "Right now, before the officials come and shoot us. The Indifferents would be expecting us and of course Orion Paratus, the leader, ya must have seen him in the game at one point, he was a very skilled knife thrower", Betty said as I remembered one of the knife-throwing men Betty had valiantly fought.

"Why can't we come and Olive? We're all Indifferents?", Levian said vexed. He had a point. "Olive doesn't have as much Indifference in her, her amount is low so she may become a liability", Brie replied. "And you and Grayson have to stay for at least another two months so your friends don't get killed when the officials look for you. They won't blame or jail you for the explosion so you're not as much at urgency but we are we need you to keep a low profile and contact so things aren't completely messed up here. Then we'll send a portal for you to join us in Ludo".

Grayson and Levian both looked like they were about to complain so I quickly called a sidebar to talk to them. "Listen guys, it's only two months and we have to do this so the federation's rule is over once and for all. For our safety and our friends", I said seriously as I gripped their arms not wanting to leave them. Grayson had proved a lot of his faults but when the time came, he had stepped up as a champ and protected Levian and me. He was still Indifferent against the federation and besides everyone was allowed to make mistakes. Levian however was going to be harder to leave. "You're not losing me Levian", I said reading his mind aptly. "You're here fighting against the federation and we'll be reunited in two months anyway, keep them safe till then", I said kissing him on the lips softly.

"We'll resume this in two months I promise", I said as he kissed my head, an unmistakable tear falling into my hair. "Continue with school then and get into college, you both need to amidst the chaos and you can't pass that opportunity. Be happy Levian". I didn't want him to mope after me or even stop dating just because I was gone, I really wanted him to make peace with everything. I hugged Grayson as well as Betty tapped on her wrist pulling a face, letting me know it was time to go. I ran towards her as she led us to the bathroom and opened a water portal in the water. "Turn the tap off as soon as we're gone", Betty said handing Brie what looked like an oxygen mask if I didn't know any better. Of course, she made water-withstanding masks. Betty was something else. We all got into the bathtub including my suitcase as Betty opened the portal for us to disappear into. It was initially rather a tight squeeze so I was hoping it would open up fast enough "I waved at Grayson and Levian who stood there solemnly waving goodbye as the portal opened wider swallowing us into our water travel destination.

"Esme", Grayson called out abruptly. "You're pure evil but you're the evil who's pure". I grinned at him fondly. "You're pure evil too Grayson, but my favourite kind of evil, you Indifferent". The bathtub vanished as our bodies hit the water with a gushing sound. I closed my eyes tightly. I wasn't ready to see what my surroundings looked like just yet. It was the most painful thing I had ever done to leave Levian behind willingly. Even Grayson and the rest of our friends but I had to. The federation being stopped was the only right thing to do before the chaos began again, before the Hallows could implement their fancy technology to start people forgetting again through their serums. It had to be done before the Hallows jumped back to their feet. Stopping them was the endgame. Before they know what we're up to. Before they make us forget yet again and continue the cycle of chaos, the connections between our past, present and future…

"Esme you need to come back to reality NOW. This has gone on for too long". All I heard was a muffled voice echoing from the ceiling. "Come BACK Esme, none of this is real". I barely remember why the voice sounded familiar but I couldn't compliment its urgency.

Part 3

The Future

CHAPTER 28

The Levian Chapter

There's so much I need to say. I don't say a lot usually so it's definite there's an absurd change in my life. Is most of what I will say even true? Probably not but I know it's how Esme remembers things and her whole story will be a fictional masterpiece rooting from her life of abuse. It'll be completely nonsensical. That's not how I would call Esme though. Esmerliah Hallows is the girl I have been erratically, profoundly and pull my brains out in love with for seven years. The moment I met her back when we were children and she would manage to sneak into my house and assure me that my parents would be fine even when they fought the federation. I'll be honest, Esme really was schizophrenic. She managed to see everything as a threat at every point and while I was still confused about her problem, I went along with her perceptions so she wouldn't freak out. When she woke up in her hospital bed, she really had been brought back to reality although Gregnitch really was the problem since he likely caused her such a terrible condition. Grayson's betrayals while terrible and manipulative had definitely not included murder in a life-sized board game but that was the only thing we played when we visited Esme. It was hard for me to recognise her condition but I did. For her to see herself as murdering a whole city was quite insane, let alone inventing people in her own little reality. I never quite understood her obsession with Captain Marvel yet she invented a whole new relative for herself. That included her fictional friend, Betty Harbor. Yet she had quite the story to tell and frankly I enjoyed the adventure of it.

She was the girl who managed to entertain the idea of a passageway connecting her house and mine but she was there for me in ways I never imagined a human capable of. She asked me what I saw in the Rotating Liah once amidst her deeply troubled phantasmagorias and while I did give her an answer, I never was direct about it but I always saw Esmerliah as my future. She was my past, my present and my desired future that I needed to alleviate the stress that regularly poured into my life. My parents' death that deeply triggered me and of course when Esme thought she died. I mean she didn't technically die, she only got lost most of her memory because of her condition but I did think I lost her. We were all miserable to bits and even sort of became distant.

We being the usual squad. Olive, Esme, Grayson, Zara, Patrick, Marshall and I. The tightest group of friends you'd ever stumble across. When we went to the pool at Patrick's party and everyone let their feelings and tempers fly high, seeing Esme rocket out of control like that made my heart crumble into bits for her. She looked like she was in so much pain and Olive may have let slip a secret Esme told her about the Hallows abusing her in front of Zara which was rather a catty move. I always felt their friendship was strained after that.

Esme was and is the strongest girl I would ever meet although she never sees herself that way. She was abused for years and years, she lived as what she imagined to be the federation's experiment for years and went through continual rounds of memory loss to forget she ever had water powers but her falsehood was how she kept herself alive however miserable it was that she truly believed it. In being a designer baby when I had to bite my lip, antagonized by myself for not telling her that designer babies were just something taught to us in our biology class at River Valley but how could I? She loves her aunt yet it's just a captain marvel figurine and when she thought she was living with her, she was the most jubilant I had seen in a while but of course I only saw her get one of her fits when they took the figuring away from her. The Rotating Liah when it was set up was one of the most ingenious inventions, she ever created in her head but I'm glad even some sort my encouragement helped her remember things more realistically if not quite. It made her remember us. Even if things were better before she remembered, before anyone remembered anything that happened after we were around 15-16. Her household was who she believed to be the Harbor federation who always ruled Kipsy City, it was terrible and seeing that my parents actually died in an accident caused by the Hallows as a threat to their daughter, it was measly that Esme blamed herself for even my fate. It was sort of curing that I befriended Esme way before albeit I'll admit initially, I was only interested in her because of her jovial demeanour. It had been so long since I had seen her completely healthy both physically and mentally.

When my parents were killed, I always thought I'd be furious at Esme but as soon as I saw her cut and bruised on one of her birthdays, I forgot it all and we would hold to our grief together in each other's arms. I've spent so much time with her during every dose of medicine she has taken since her accident but her episodes were always going to show up. I think everyone in Kipsy and Abilo heard about it in the papers, Esme's ingenious imagination perceived it as her aunt's home town being taken over by the Hallows a few months ago as well before their game. I never expected to be termed as an Indifferent, a radical that didn't succumb to their 'memory serums' and games to keep control but I should have known considering my parents did die at their hands alongside some of their other monstrosities they committed towards Esme, it's no surprise she saw her own doll as a fugitive turned ally. Betty Harbor never left her side.

So yes, when I did refresh Esme's memories using the 'Rotating Liah', I reminisced with memories like this but my favourite had to ironically be the one after my parents died when Esme hugged me close and I would never feel that warmth with anyone else ever. Especially at the times we live in. When Patrick had one of his parties on his next birthday, I was impeccably angry that Esme seemed to like Grayson. The guitar playing titan from hell who likes calling me, 'Lev'. I like Grayson but he is the last person to ever be faultless. It triggered me to a greater level when that lousy little piece of work chose to date Zara instead and broke Esme's heart.

I tried to punch him once for that but he caught my fist knowingly and admitted he was wrong yet he knew I was only angry because I was the one who wanted to be with her. I hadn't any intentions at the time knowing how complicated

Esme's life was but it did dawn on me that I may want that. Of course, Grayson is a manipulative jerk but he's intuitive and sadly his villainous behaviour wasn't ever a hallucination.

He gave me effortless words of encouragement and I was determined to win her over as something more than a friend someday. I knew it and I knew she did too. We always had our moments so when we thought she was dead after her schizophrenic episode post her asylum visit, I was heartbroken. Zara and Grayson broke up and that's when I saw something I never caught my eye on. The glib in Grayson seemed to have dimmed out. I could see he missed her dreadfully as I observed him. Grayson and Esme had always been close but I knew he didn't know her as well as I did. Nobody knew her like I did. Why was he so embittered? Olive was a great comfort to me at this time and I felt guilty seeking her comfort throughout because I knew Esme would have been stricken to see Olive and I getting too closed. She would loathe to be replaced. I could see her hate it at Patrick's party when she was drunk and in a wicked way, I enjoyed it. It had broken my heart to know that she liked Grayson and when Olive saw me aching, she went and confessed to Grayson that Esme liked him. It was a downright malicious move and I was awfully annoyed at Olive but I knew it was in Esme's best interest. I think that was the second strain in their friendship but life moved on from there.

We lived in grief for a whole year when Esme was actually still alive and having a good life in her head with the aunt who rescued her as a child. We all thought we lost her and wile I don't admit it, we have and we won't have her other than at tiny glimpses of time like an old buffering laptop.

Esme had never once mentioned how it all fell apart from her after boarding school. There was a time she believed that her aunt Brie couldn't keep her and Esme was sent to boarding school as our school had a section to accommodate people with her condition yet she never once mentioned her. She never mentioned a lot of things come to think of it. Her infatuation for Grayson, her life at Abilo, her hallucinations of her aunt, that weird doll/friend of hers called Betty, her loathing for Olive although I cracked that puzzle and even her obsession with water powers. The Hallows used several ways of torture on her to make her forget any sort of horrible thing they did to her that would cost them legal trouble but they were never perfectly skilled enough to make people forget everything for long periods of time. The truth always slipped out and people like me and even Olive always knew of the truth. Esme always acted like she was in a hurry to get on with life as if she was scared that people would remember that she was the monster who killed all those people in the city when she was actually suffering badly. It was always the Hallows responsible. Before they remembered anything, she would try get as much as possible out of her life and when she did explode again at Patrick's party, she was shipped away without saying goodbye until it was announced that she was dead.

I was confused out of my wits when she arrived from that same passageway to my house one day clutching at her doll and ranting about me using the Rotating Liah again to show her all her memories. All I could do was feed her and tell her all she forgot or the true version of events. She was alive, somewhere hidden under all those psychotic flames of bubbled confusion that confined her in her own, once witty brain. I was glad that we still had that connection and I tried my best to remind her of everything despite the tears that would prick the sides of my eyes. She looked fiercely strong despite her weakness, how she escaped that hospital even once was wonderous but I just needed to hold her for the last time in case her condition did pronounce her as dead. It meant a lot that she was still fighting it. Patrick's latest party that was with her was the first party we had since she disappeared the previous year. I wasn't going to go considering she wouldn't be there but as soon as she happened to be alive and safe, I drove her straight down to Saltlake to Patrick's house. Emotions were rather high that day for it was quite a reunion, she seemed almost normal at the time.

A part of me selfishly wishes I never took her there or I would walk into Patrick's balcony to see my heart shattered in a million pieces as I walked in on Grayson and Esme kissing. I never expected to see that but I couldn't say I was surprised. I always knew Grayson was afraid to love Esme more than he liked Zara. Zara was a sweet girl but she didn't have the fire Esme did. The strong bursts of emotion that drove Esme to fight for the ones she loved and against the torment she faced every day. He was afraid of her episodes to be sure but Grayson had always been selfish. Esme had changed a lot since the last time and her newfound control over her insanity that she so flawlessly delivered was definitely a trait I would remember in her favour. I was disheartened and a little betrayed but I couldn't stand in her way. I loved the girl yet she seemed to love Grayson. Worst part is she seemed almost completely sane.

A lot happened since then, I remember Esme falling screaming to the ground with a knife around Grayson's hand screaming about Grayson stabbing me in her game of the Indifferents, we were forced to call the Hallows and her hospital ward letting her awaken to reality and remember everything, it was the first time since her accident she found herself in normalcy despite her believing everything to be a lie. I wanted to leave without a word but after holding Esme in the hospital after Gregnitch Hallows had assaulted her. I had never been that flamed, that furious, that wrecked before. I wanted to kill him with my own bare hands, strangle him to death. I couldn't ever leave her after that, it didn't matter how much it pained me.

I was there for her every day since then until almost two months ago she fell into a coma right after another Ludo game. Grayson and I had to leave for college in around two more weeks as we focused on school instead and all the reporters and policemen made their inquiries about what really happened at Esme's accident and about the attack at the same hospital after Gregnitch had been arrested. Esme did manage to choose me over Grayson in the end but all it cost was her healthy lifeline. I stayed in Kipsy on guarded watch and focusing on school and she was no doubt off investigating the source of her water magic in her endless dreams. I knew she felt safe there and that she'd return again. She was with her doll Betty. The holy trinity team I seemed to miraculously been forced into with Esme and Grayson was getting quite tiring and now neither of us ever managed to sort ourselves out.

Grayson played really sad songs on his guitar sometimes or really violent ones, both of which took me by surprise. He had moved in with me after asking his parents so we could visit Emse together at the hospital before her brain scans. We both really prayed every day that she would wake up as we talked normally in front of her to keep her dreaming. As long as she dreamt, she would remain alive. We did become closer as a result. It irked me when he made jokes about kissing Esme and very inappropriate intimacy ones and despite how many times, I would tell him that I didn't care of what times they had together, he always enlightens me all the same. He's better than having no company when we're grieving the same ultimate loss.

Esme really worked well at highlighting surprises for other people. I would never have thought I would be living with Grayson and it was astonishingly bearable even if I wanted to kick him in a place, he wouldn't want to be kicked in. Talking about Esme also sometimes helped alleviate the tension we were constantly in and we always try keep things positive despite how bitter they could become.

Another thing I never knew about Esme was how much writing really helped her. She mentioned something about the asylum she was in once and how they mentioned writing in a journal to remember everything she could and get her feelings out at one point but I never knew she actually attempted to do that. I never knew I would be writing in her journal either considering she left it behind. That was the only remnants of her. She took her suitcase but she left the journal. I'll admit my curiosity illegally peer pressured me into reading a few of the entries she wrote as she titled everything in parts. The past where she mentioned her experiences in the Rotating Liah and life in Abilo, her present which was the game and some of the most recent memories and her future that she had left blank.

Writing in that section is extremely restorative of my mental state. It makes me prove to her that I'm willing to wait for her until she awakens so I can be with her again. It makes me believe I'm her future and no hallucinations can take that away from me. Esme might have continued writing to keep her memories intact since information dramatizes itself in her brain and she could have a direct source when she remembers but she needs to know how much I love and respect her.

I always have. I love her silence, the way her blue eyes that match the sea shine up in golden light when she flexes her powers. I love her radiance when she fights against the federation and the way she always understands me. I love her long hair and the way her nose scrunches up when something weirds her out. She's brave, she always jumps back and I love that spirit she has. I miss her every day and although I expected the two months to be hard, it still hit me terribly, it's one of the most painful things I've had to do. Saying goodbye to her even if I know I'll see her again. Losing her is terrifying. I can't wait to seize that moment with her when I finally see her and wrap her in my arms and kiss her on the top of her head and breathe in her hair that smells like fresh leaves in spring. I want those moments before we have to fight again, before we remember our goals. If she ever forgets, I would remind her with my presence and just bask in the serenity of that moment before she remembers everything again. I want to just see her smile and laugh and brush away those beautiful tears from her eyes that look like raindrops on the most heavenly days before the world remembers to throw obstacles at us once more. No, I *crave* for those moments with her again, I *desire* making new memories with her in the future. She's my *past*, my *present*, and my *future*. I want to remind her of all of those things before I'm another Indifferents forgotten by her again. Before we are reminded of the game that caused the rebellion's hope. It's really just a game of a complex brain turned dysfunctional because of the war it has indulged in. Before they remember where she got her sanity from. I just want to be with her *before I can lose her again. Before she remembers* that this is all just a schizophrenic episode that completely nettled me when I read it. All she needs to remember is that I love her despite any illness that may contain her and therefore I continued her story. Her version of the Ludo board game and her recollection of me in her story. Despite it all being just another game of memory.

Which Indifferent are YOU?

Are you emotional and brave like Esme? Are you strong and loving like Aunt Brie? Nifty and loyal like Levian? Maybe resourceful and musical like Grayson? Or passionate and aggressive like Betty?

1. **You're in a life and death game of snakes and ladders. What do you choose to do?**
    a. Struggle to control your emotions as you shield yourself with magic?
    b. Give your loved one's snakebite antidote while you sacrifice yourself?
    c. Protect your beloved with logical solutions and self-made engineered weapons?
    d. Manipulate your way to win and backstab your friends?
    e. Kill everyone around you and rationally use shapeshifting to win?

2. **You return to River Valley Highschool after your memory was wiped. What are you like now?**
    a. Confused, emotional, and determined to win your life back?
    b. Finding your way around patiently through other people's memories?
    c. Grateful to see your loved one, inventing a memory restoring machine to remember your past?

d. You use your charms and looks to seduce the person who would give you most power and success

e. You won't return to high school and find a way to destroy the system that fed you the memory serum in the first place.

3. **If you had to choose one person to save from the Hallows, who would it be?**

   a. Everyone, you feel guilty that you're the reason everyone is in danger.

   b. Esme, you're motherly and believe that everyone deserves a second chance.

   c. You try protect everyone but take extra precautions to save Esme, your damsel in distress.

   d. Yourself, you prioritize your safety but use other people to help you.

   e. Nobody, you believe everybody deserves to die.

4. **What are your best qualities?**

   a. You're courageous, forgiving, and expressive.

   b. You're insightful, protective of your loved ones, and strong.

   c. You're intelligent, handy, and the most affectionate person ever.

   d. You're musically gifted, attractive, and rather shrewd.

   e. You're whimsical, fierce, and independent.

5. **What do you despise in your life/fear it happening to you?**

    a. Mental illnesses like Schizophrenia/PTSD/ depression/Insomnia/Eating disorders.

    b. Losing your family or having them find out your dangerous secrets.

    c. Jealousy since the one you love fancies your best friend despite giving them your all.

    d. Not having any power, and feeling any emotions. (You think emotions make you weak)

    e. Getting punished for all your crimes and murders.

6. **What is your ideal type/lover?**

    a. Charming, musical, and attractive. You like someone who's dominant and less emotional.

    b. You don't care as long as you have children you can love and protect.

    c. Your childhood best friend. Someone emotional, and brave who shares your musical taste.

    d. As long as you're getting physical action with someone attractive and vocal, it doesn't matter.

    e. Anyone who can handle your fierce passion, and replicate it.

7. **What future plans do you have for yourself?**

    a. Explore the field of marine biology/sciences as you learnt to control your emotions and powers.

b. Explore the culinary arts and live a nice peaceful, loving life with your family in a beautiful house and town.

c. Explore engineering with a top university degree as you enjoy partying, and dating the person you've loved for ages.

d. Acquiring all the power from your current government as you take over and rule politically.

e. Remaining a fugitive and using your water powers to your advantage to get whatever you want.

Mostly A's: You're Esmerliah Hallows! You've led a difficult life of abuse and trauma as you were genetically manufactured as a weapon to control Kipsy City by the Hallows. You have destructive water magic that is often out of your control and has made you a monster in the eyes of the city folk for mass genocide. You're expressive and emotional as you struggle to control your emotions and magic. You're also brave and determined to help restore your city despite all the challenges you've faced but are often oblivious to love.

Mostly B's: You're Aunt Brie! You were quite the normal woman until you found the magical child being physically abused by a strange man. You bravely rescued her from there despite a whole city wanting to kill her and kept her as your adopted child. You love cooking, baking, and decorating your house. You treat everyone equally and never refrain from using your insight and kindness wherever you can. You're strong and you always find your way while protecting those you love even if you have to convince a whole city.

Mostly C's: You're Levian! You're clever, academic, and handy as you create useful tools like the Rotating Liah to help you and your loved ones in times of crisis. You're in love with your childhood best friend Esme and unwilling to hide your jealousy when she chooses your best friend Grayson over you. You're loyal and caring to those you love and never afraid to stick up for them. Your brains ensure you a wonderful future.

Mostly D's: You're Grayson! You're extremely attractive with a soft musical side and unmatched banter. You're a genius at the guitar. You desire power and aren't afraid to use your resourcefulness to get your own way. You're often cunning, manipulative, and dangerous when you're achieving your goals but can turn out to be a true romantic. You betray your friends including Levian and Esme but come around to fight for what you think is right.

Mostly E's: You're Betty Harbor! You're a force. You were created by the Hallow Federation as a killer and become a fugitive, wanted for all the people you've killed. You're fearless and unpredictable, unique in your way of thinking. You're extremely passionate about what you love doing, especially in your shape shifting water powers and your mission in taking down the Hallows and the federation. You're beautiful in all your shapes and put up a good fight. You have a hard time letting people in although you have a good heart and embrace your allies just like you terminate your enemies.

Before They Remember Questionnaire Survey:

My results have confirmed by a normal teenage, populated target group that each person embodied each character of mine in different ways. Some face the same mental disorders such as Esmerliah herself which shows the strain of mental disability in a conformed dystopian society. While Before They Remember explores concepts of Dystopian control and the misuse of genetically modified equipment, the ethical consideration is a broad concept to follow considering that children are used as human, shape shifted weapons to aid the Hallow's dictatorship. By conducting a survey of 10 initial classmates of mine, each person responded to a different character trait which helped them analyze their own disabilities, characters based on mental disadvantages that further allows self-cognizance. When each of these character's journey through their redemptions, their self-discovered journeys as Indifferents or side characters, they establish their own values and roles in self-discovered learning of their ideals.

www.ingramcontent.com/pod-product-compliance
Lightning Source LLC
LaVergne TN
LVHW091305150826
845673LV00006B/1546

* 9 7 9 8 8 9 0 2 6 4 8 7 9 *